THE CHOSEN SEVEN

best wishes
from *Gill* x

GILL D. ANDERSON

Disclaimer

The Chosen Seven is a work of fiction. Any names, characters, businesses, agencies, organisations, places, events, locales, and incidents are either the products of the author's imagination or used in a fictitious manner. Any resemblance to actual persons, living or dead, or actual events is purely coincidental.

To the many South Australia Police officers who have become my friends and family, the characters in this book in no way resemble any police officers known to me.

The Chosen Seven © Gill D. Anderson 2019

ISBN: 978-1-925962-77-2 (paperback)

Cataloguing-in-Publication information for this title is listed with the National Library of Australia.

Published in Australia by Gill D. Anderson and InHouse Publishing.
www.inhousepublishing.com.au
Printed in Australia by InHouse Print & Design.

This book is dedicated to my colleagues at The Department for Child Protection in Adelaide. I am so lucky to work with such supportive and encouraging staff. I believe this book would not be possible without you all pushing me forward and being understanding about me taking time off at the crucial manuscript appraisal and editing stages. I am grateful to each and every one of you for supporting my dual career and suffering me when I am tired from writing the night before.

Yours gratefully, Gill xx

PROLOGUE

Saturday 6 April 2019, 7.00pm, Eat Street, Seminyak, Bali

Farzad Abed felt hot and bothered. Sweat poured relentlessly down his imposing heavyset frame. Farzad had some idea about what had to happen, but the exact circumstances and the people involved were yet to be determined. Despite the sunset just over an hour before, it was impossible for him to cool down due to the intense humidity. Farzad scanned his surroundings as he walked by the overwhelming array of enticing menus outside each eatery on the popular Eat Street near Seminyak Square. The heat was getting to him and the anger that constantly simmered at the surface of his mind was becoming dangerously close to making him explode.

Farzad would make his mark on the world, of that he was sure. He was mindful, however, that his indecisive, impatient and flighty nature might cause him to rush things and foil his plan. Being erratic was his downfall, so he tried to remind himself of this. He would know when the right place and time were presented to him. He had an important message to convey to the world and the perfect people would need to be chosen to help him ensure it was spread across the globe. There would be a sign from the universe, and he would feel it in his bones, in his very fibres.

He darted into a large restaurant with an expansive outdoor eating area. Several holidaymakers sat sipping indulgent cocktails, enjoying a casual al fresco dinner while spending their hard-earned wages on their annual holiday indulgences. Despite the relaxed vibe of the eatery with its colourful umbrellas and benches scattered with large inviting cushions, the relentless stream of taxis and motorbikes thundering past was in direct contrast to the vibe the establishment attempted to emulate. A young Australian couple became aware of the tall heavyset man sitting at the table next to them. His thick black curls were damp with sweat and his sunglasses had slipped down his nose. He sat at the table to their left, his legs spread wide, his gut hanging down between them and placed his sunglasses on top of his head. The couple paused their conversation momentarily and noted the man's strange vibe and penetrating stare.

In unison, the couple attempted to exchange polite but uneasy smiles with their new dining neighbour, who did not smile back. Instead, he stared menacingly at them. They tried to resume their conversation under the steady glare of this strange man, who sat extremely close to them. Had he moved his table closer in an attempt to join them? The female pitied him and thought perhaps he was just lonely. In stark contrast, the male's antenna for weirdos had been activated and alarm bells were starting to go off in his head.

A petite Balinese waitress appeared and presented a menu to Farzad, a warm welcoming smile lighting up her dainty features. Abruptly, Farzad stood up and flipped the menu out of the waitress's hands upwards into the air. He stared at her, his teeth bared, his eyes darting wildly around the venue. On a whim, he thundered towards the exit while muttering incoherently to himself. The waitress staggered backwards in shock, an alarmed expression on her face. Picking up the menu from the ground, her gaze followed the retreating man who had taken off down the street. Sometimes tourists were so strange, she thought. Once she was sure he had left the vicinity, she let out a sigh of relief and resumed her duties. However, she could not shake off the gut feeling that she had just got off lightly somehow. Instinctively she knew the strange man intended to cause harm and she was thankful she hadn't been his next victim.

Farzad was fizzing mad when he returned to the mayhem of Eat Street. He grimaced and considered how those fuckers had gotten off lightly tonight. He had not executed his plan; not only were the patrons in that eatery not worthy of hearing his message to the world, but in addition, none of them had shown any leadership potential. They were all pathetic weaklings, not noble enough to be a part of his cause. Little did the people in that eatery know that his change of heart had spared them their lives tonight. They would live another day; thanks to the pitiful couple he had made eye contact with. They were too desperately boring to be a part of the fun and games he had planned.

The other pedestrians tried to avoid Farzad as he marched along the narrow pavement without stopping to let anyone pass him. His girth and penetrating eyes made the other tourists uneasy and no one challenged him when he shoved past them, knocking bags from shoulders and elbowing people in the chest, causing them to yelp in pain. Even the groups of Balinese girls outside the many massage parlours who automatically called out 'massage' to anyone who looked remotely like a tourist knew instinctively not to offer their services to this odd-looking man.

Farzad reached his hotel and quickened his pace as he stormed past the bemused concierge straight into the vacant lift. He exited the lift on the third floor, turned left and thundered along the corridor as fast as his huge frame would allow. Upon reaching his room, he became flustered when his first two attempts to insert the key card failed. Finally, he managed to time it correctly and the green light indicated he could enter the room. His face was beetroot with rage, as he stood silently in the dark, allowing the cranked-up air conditioning to blast some welcome cold air onto his sweaty frame. After a few minutes, he felt calmer. Like a zombie, he stared blindly into space for a while. He had no idea how much time had passed when he eventually sat ramrod straight on the end of the king-size bed.

Farzad could not have articulated his thoughts even if he tried. He tried to remember why he was in Bali and then it came to him. His intention was to harm Westerners much like in the Bali bombings of 2002. He wanted to do something on a much smaller scale but equally as horrifying. Somehow, it hadn't felt right, and he would fly back to Adelaide tomorrow without completing his mission. Eventually he grew tired and allowed himself to fall backwards onto the bed. Finally, when he succumbed to sleep, he surmised that perhaps he would have better luck in executing his plan in the near future. Tonight, had not been the right time after all.

CHAPTER 1

Friday 17 May 2019, 5.00pm

Jacob Brown swaggered up the driveway of his parents' modest detached red-brick two-storey home. At twenty-three years of age, he was in his prime and was looking mighty fine, if he did say so himself. He had just finished four back-to-back personal training sessions at the local gym with his loyal clients. Jacob loved his job as a personal trainer but often he would vague out and not be watching their form due to catching a glimpse of himself in the many mirrors around the expansive gym. It was hard not to be distracted by his own incredible physique, bleached-blond surfer hair and those baby blue eyes. He marvelled at every toned inch of his splendidness each day and definitely fancied himself more than his girlfriend, Layla, did. He had reached adulthood during the social media boom and was no stranger to posting numerous selfies of his chiselled and muscular frame on a regular basis.

Jacob had built his biceps up to such a degree that his mother, Jackie, told him he looked like he had a roll of carpet under each arm whenever he walked towards her. His dad, Colin, often joked that he looked like he might topple over due to being so top-heavy. This annoyed Jacob to no end, and he intended to move out soon because Jackie in particular was becoming rather annoying with her comments about him fancying himself. Jacob regularly fought over the bathroom mirror with Jackie and his fourteen-year-old sister Leonie. Colin was the only member of the household who couldn't give a rat's ass about his appearance and Jacob secretly thought his dad was a fat slob. Jacob was determined he would not end up that way, hence his fitness obsession.

Jacob entered the family home and shouted out hi to whoever was home. Normally he could smell dinner cooking, but no pleasing aromas were forthcoming. 'What's for tea, Mum?' he called out as he shrugged his gym bag off his shoulder and placed it on the hall table. Jacob caught sight of himself in the hall mirror and made a mental note to start using eye cream. He was sure he could see the first signs of crow's feet.

He heard the distinct drawl of a moody female voice directly above him. 'I'm afraid there will be no dinner tonight,' the voice said slowly and deliberately. He looked up to see a dainty female form lying on her front with her face propped on her hands, her elbows digging into the carpet, peering down from the upstairs landing. Her legs were bent upwards from the knees and she crisscrossed her feet back and forth in an agitated childlike manner.

Jacob rolled his eyes and replied, 'What the hell? What's been going on to cause a dinner strike this time?' A moody ponytailed face stared back down at him, chewing bubble gum noisily like a petulant child. Instead of replying, she blew a huge bubble until it popped. *This behaviour is so childish,* thought Jacob. From his fourteen-year-old sister Leonie, this immature crap could almost be expected. However, his forty-five-year-old *mother,* who was old enough to know better, was the one behaving like a juvenile. Jacob sighed and speed-dialled his favourite Italian restaurant, Alessandro's Cucina, to order his usual low carb pasta dish to take away. The food was amazing, and it was well worth making the trip into the city to collect it. Unfortunately, the owner was a bit old school and hadn't picked up on the concept of home delivery in the form of Uber Eats yet.

Jacob could only surmise that his dad had done something to piss his mum off again, which had prompted her tantrum and consequent cooking strike. He popped his head around the lounge room door and saw his dad lying stretched out on the sofa, legs crossed and hands behind his head. He spotted Jacob as he entered and nodded moodily in his direction.

'What the hell have you been fighting about now?' Jacob frowned at his dad; frustration etched on his handsome face.

'I told her that her breath stunk and she went berserk,' replied Colin in a monotone voice. Jacob screwed up his face in disgust and shook his head.

'You guys are pathetic, as if you would fall out about *that*.'

Colin sat up and folded his arms across his chest defiantly. 'Your mother's response was that having bad breath was better than being a fat bastard, so I told her to shove her dinner up her arse.' Colin paused. 'That's why your sister has gone to stay at her friend's house tonight. So, you will have to fend for yourself given that dinner is not happening,' Colin pouted.

Jacob could not be bothered to get into it with either parent. They had regressed back to kindergarten behaviour. 'Bye, Dad,' he said in a flat voice, barely concealing his annoyance. He turned on his heel to leave the lounge room.

Jackie heard her son open the front door. 'Oi, where you going? You only just got home!' she yelled from her spot on the landing above.

'I'm going out to pick up a takeaway from Alessandro's Cucina since I'm clearly not getting fed here!' fumed Jacob, and he slammed the front door behind him.

As he unlocked his car, he could hear his mum yelling down to his dad, 'You're a prick, Colin!' Jacob didn't know whether to laugh or cry as he drove off to collect his takeaway.

Jacob felt pensive while he sat in the peak hour traffic. His friends found his parents' little fallouts hilarious and were always entertained when they put on a show in their presence. Quite frankly, though, Jacob and Leonie were over it. *Weren't adults meant to be responsible role models?* Whenever Jacob said this to Jackie, she would burst out into that derisive laugh of hers and snort, 'We are all just winging it mate, adulting is overrated!' Jacob was keen to move out but he'd looked at the cost involved and realised he would no longer be able to spend his money on designer clothes and fancy holidays. While he was tired of his parents' bullshit, he'd resigned himself to the fact that he'd have to suffer them a bit longer. His long-term aim was to become a personal trainer in Hollywood. He could picture himself on a movie set putting hot actresses through their paces in between scenes.

Jacob's stomach rumbled and he put his foot on the gas. The sooner he got his takeaway, the sooner he could fill his belly. He'd never admit to anyone how hungry he was or how quickly he intended to shovel his takeaway down his throat. Discipline was everything in the gym world and it wouldn't do to be caught gorging.

CHAPTER 2

Friday 17 May 2019, 5.35pm

Regina Terry sat at a table for two at Alessandro's Cucina. She looked at her watch and took note of the time. Her date was already five minutes late for pre-dinner drinks and she was getting agitated. She hoped Australian men weren't all dumb pricks like they were back in New York. Given that she'd already 'checked in' to the venue on Facebook, the whole world would know her current location soon (and hopefully guess that she was on a date). Regina was a robust African American woman in her late thirties. Her longest relationship had lasted nine months. The reason for these short-lived affairs, according to Regina, was that she took no shit from anybody. Regina's unfortunate ex-partners would likely beg to differ and say the breakups were due to Regina being an overbearing possessive psycho.

Regina had recently arrived in Australia on a Temporary Skill Shortage visa due to the demand for software and applications programmers. She had jumped at the chance when her boss in New York suggested she go overseas for a year. He had connections in South Australia and put in a good word for her. He secretly hoped that it would not come back to bite him on the bum as the result of Regina going off on one of her renowned tangents. Instead of realising that her boss wanted a break from her overbearing personality, Regina saw it as a ticket to meet the man of her dreams. When she first landed on Australian soil, however, she had been somewhat disappointed to note that there was not a single Paul Hogan lookalike in sight.

Regina had only recently become acquainted with the Tinder dating app and to her delight she'd stumbled across a local South Australian man named Gary Bartlett who wore a fedora hat and leather waistcoat in his profile picture. He wasn't quite Crocodile Dundee to look at, but she acknowledged she was no Halle Berry either. They'd begun flirting in earnest by exchanging various risqué texts and photos, but Regina was crafty enough to only send carefully angled pictures of herself. She knew she was a big girl and wasn't trying to hide the fact, but all the same, she felt that certain men who would initially be put off by her thunder thighs would eventually come around when they were charmed by her larger-than-life personality.

Regina enjoyed being independent and if the truth be known, she wasn't necessarily on the lookout for a life partner. If it happened, it happened, and if it didn't, it didn't. Most of her friends were in awe of her ability not to become attached or needy where men were concerned. Regina would shrug nonchalantly and brag that she had the ability to shed men as often as a snake sheds its skin. Sometimes she felt her pragmatic approach to relationships was traditionally male. More often than not, she would eye up her next suitor with a view to tiring them out with a marathon sex session before 'chewing them up and spitting them out', as she referred to it. She liked wild sex and plenty of it. Men were often surprised at how agile she was despite her ample build. Regina chuckled and considered how some of her dates must have felt when she'd treated them like a booty call. She justified this by the assumption that they'd probably made some poor unsuspecting woman feel used in much the same way at some point, so she was simply there to dish out their karma.

Regina gave a loud snort when she thought back to her last drunken sexual encounter with a bearded truck driver back in New York the week before she left for Australia. She had flung him around the bedroom like a ragdoll as they tried almost every sex position she knew of. In the morning he'd rolled over and asked with a smile if she was making him breakfast. In response, she'd yelled, 'Do I look like yo motha? I'm not atcha beck and call, dude. Get yo ho ass outta ma Goddamn bed and don't come back!' When the poor guy threw on his clothes and slunk out into the bustling street, she'd opened the window and jeered down at him, 'I ain't *nobody's* bitch and I ain't makin no man any damn eggs in the mornin'!' Utterly mortified, he didn't dare to look up at her. He was too busy thinking, *Once again I've attracted a psycho bitch, when I will I ever learn?* A teenage boy watched the whole exchange with interest and feeling intrigued, he'd glanced up to see where the furious female voice was coming from. Regina was about to give him a piece of her mind for being so nosy when it occurred to her that the reason the boy appeared to be glued to the spot was because she'd gotten carried away and yelled out of the window whilst naked. She looked down and sure enough she'd acted without thinking. It was her worst trait.

Muttering obscenities, she'd slammed the window shut, yanked the blinds down, then stomped off to have a shower, her large breasts bouncing along the way. She looked down at them and tutted. It was likely that half her street had seen these precious babies by now. It was time she asserted more self-control and stopped being so quick to react but yelling out of the window was a defence mechanism from her childhood; she'd always done it to scare off the crooks in the Bronx. As the shower washed over her, Regina smirked. She was close to forty years old and it was unlikely she'd change now. Thinking about the priceless look on the teenage boy's face, she burst into a throaty cackle while she lathered up her ample body. *I could have made his day and let him motorboat these babies.*

·· • ● • ··

Regina's thoughts abruptly returned to the present and her eyes refocused on the entrance to the restaurant. She was not the most patient person in the world and certainly wouldn't sit around if this Tinder dude kept her waiting. She *had* insisted on an early dinner and he *did* have to travel from the other side of town so she tried to be reasonable and take that into consideration. Given that there was still no sign of him, she took out her compact mirror and studied her round dark face and beady brown eyes for a few seconds before applying her favourite Sephora gooey candy pink lip gloss to her generous mouth. She smacked her thick lips together to even out the gloss and shook out her afro curls with a confident air. Liking what she saw, she nodded at her reflection with self-satisfied smirk.

As Regina snapped the compact mirror shut, she considered with glee how sassy and bold she was and did not suffer fools gladly. These thoughts caused her wide nostrils to flare and her huge bosom to heave up and down while she became increasingly agitated with every passing minute. *I ain't waitin any longer for no stoopid dude to show up!* Regina was about to stomp towards the exit in disgust when her mobile phone ringing distracted her. Her brother Zion was calling from back home in New York. Regina sat back down to take the call as she got too breathless when she tried to walk and talk at the same time. It would buy the asshole she was meeting an extra few minutes. *If he was lucky...*

CHAPTER 3

Friday 17 May 2019, 5.50pm

Levi Haines was tired. She'd been at work since 7.00am and barely stopped for a toilet break all day. At twenty-eight years old, she had already climbed the corporate ladder to a director position in the Attorney-General's Department. Levi had worked hard to gain her position but was struggling with the male chauvinist pigs that she worked alongside. Levi presented as sleek, elegant and well-dressed. She was petite in both height and build with large brown eyes, olive skin and a mane of long, glossy chestnut coloured hair. Unfortunately, the frumpy older females in her office allowed her beauty and brains to make them feel inadequate. While she loved her job, every day was a battle due to her lack of allies, and it was becoming exhausting. It was Friday evening and all Levi wanted was to go home to her husband Ben and their one-year-old daughter, Charlie. Her boss, Bill Walker, had other ideas, however. Netflix, wine and cuddles with her loved ones would have to wait. Bill informed her that they *had to* talk about work-related projections and figures and he was *far* too busy during business hours, hence the impending dinner.

Levi knew perfectly well that Bill had other intentions and his aim was to have time alone with her. The feeling was not mutual but being a people pleaser was one of her few flaws. Levi managed to keep her thoughts to herself but the truth was that she could not stand Bill or anything he stood for. In her view, he was a misogynistic prick with no morals or values. To make matters worse, he had bad manners and was an all-round slimy, manipulative toad. Levi was well aware however, that if she was to get him offside, he could make her position redundant and get rid of her at any time. She had worked too hard for too long to allow that to happen. Levi sat with her head in her hands at her desk while she waited for Bill to come and escort her across the road to Alessandro's Cucina for dinner. *Please be over quickly. I hate business dinners. This should be family time.*

·· • ● • ··

Bill Walker was one of the rudest men walking the Earth. He'd caught the tram to work that morning because he knew he would be wining and dining Levi after work. His precious red Ferrari F40 was staying safely undercover in his garage for today. There was no way he would drink and drive behind the wheel of *that* precious toy. The tram stop was particularly busy that morning and despite being last to arrive, he impatiently shoved his way on when the tram pulled in, pushing in front of the other passengers in an urgent manner. Bill practically ran to one of the few vacant seats despite noting an elderly man with a walking stick and a young woman who was clearly in the late stages of pregnancy and not quick enough on her feet.

A gothic-looking teenage girl standing next to the pregnant lady glared at Bill, her black kohl-rimmed eyes closely watching him as her earphones blasted dark emo music into her ears. She hated Bill on sight. What she saw was a ruddy faced, sandy haired old dude with a craggy lined face and a messed up attitude. His face reminded her of a smashed crab. This was in stark contrast to the reflection Bill had seen in his en suite mirror before he left home. Feeling confident about his ability to charm Levi, he'd nodded approvingly at his boyish good looks and full head of hair while he dabbed on some Tom Ford Noir de Noir aftershave before heading out the front door. Bill reckoned he looked at least a decade younger than his fifty-five years. No one dared tell him he was delusional.

Bill was still reeling from his recent divorce from wife number three. Not because he missed her as such, but because he'd thought she was different and stupidly hadn't asked her to sign a pre-nuptial agreement. As he was worth a few million dollars, it probably wasn't the smartest thing he'd ever done. Bill did not possess an ounce of reflective capacity and it never occurred to him for even one second that he was the common denominator in the breakdown of all of his relationships. He had been an absent husband and father much of the time, and as a result, meaningful relationships were non-existent in his life. Instead of analysing why this might be, he preferred to wallow in self-pity. His children had grown up without much input from him and during his last conversation with his eldest son, he'd told Bill solemnly that 'you reap what you sow'. Bill had been livid at that comment after all the money he'd forked out over the years for his kids' private schooling, trips away, sporting clubs and whatever else they clicked their fingers for. His son had shaken his head sadly and walked away. *It is pointless arguing with the ignorant; they merely see what they want to see.* Bill could not compute that children need their parents' time, love and wise counsel above anything else in life.

When Bill was going through his first divorce to Donna, they'd had a particularly ferocious argument whereby she'd screamed at him, 'Do you even know anything about your children? Such as their favourite foods, their talents and their hobbies?' Bill stared at her blankly as though she was talking a foreign language. The final straw and consequent catalyst for the divorce occurred when their son Liam had a severe allergic reaction to another child's peanut butter sandwich at school and his EpiPen had to be administered. The teacher was unable to get a hold of Donna initially and therefore contacted Bill, who'd barked at her that he was far too busy to deal with it and wouldn't be coming to take Liam for a routine medical check-up despite it being an agreed component of his medical care plan held by the school. Bill was more interested in demonising the mother who'd allowed her child to sneak in a peanut butter sandwich despite the school's strict 'no nuts' policy. The child in question had made the sandwich without their mum's knowledge and was now scarred for life due to the craggy faced, sandy haired angry old man who'd burst into the classroom a few days later and bellowed at him. Bill had been asked to leave and was escorted from the school grounds, then banned from returning. His children suffered all manner of taunts and jibes about the incident and never seemed able to live it down. Any resentment they already harboured for their father only increased tenfold following that mortifying episode.

· · ● · ·

It was almost time for the greatly anticipated dinner. Bill smirked to himself as he closed down his computer for the weekend and reached for his navy suit jacket that matched so well with his beige chinos. Bill wrongly assumed that the women at work secretly admired his sense of style and distinguished looks. The reality was that the women sniggered during their lunch breaks about the navy and beige outfit combination that seemed to be a bit of a cliché for the men over fifty in the corporate world. As far as they were concerned, it was an absolute turn-off and was the most unimaginative outfit a man could possibly come up with. Bill flicked off an imaginary speck of dust from his lapel. He surmised that he didn't give a shit that Levi was dining with him under duress. If she wanted to earn her corporate stripes, she would need to do all that he required of her. He gave his hair a quick comb through, then rubbed his hands together in anticipation. Bill did not care about Levi's drip of a husband or bratty kid missing out on family time with her. He had been there and done that. Happy families were *so* overrated. Knowing she was married added to the fun of the chase. He *would* have his wicked way with her. It was not a matter of *if*, more a matter of *when*.

At 5.55pm Bill and Levi arrived at Alessandro's Cucina and were shown to an intimate booth for two by a demure looking dark-skinned waitress. Levi was filled with dread, and Bill in direct contrast was filled with excitement. The evening was certainly about to take an unexpected turn for both of them.

CHAPTER 4

Friday 17 May 2019, 5.57pm

Jagriti Ghoshal was an unassuming nineteen-year-old Indian girl with a softly spoken voice and quiet demeanour. She looked younger than her years due to her small slender body showing no signs of having ever been through puberty. The long black plait of hair that hung down her back only added to her girlish look. Jagriti had a mature outlook and was a popular waitress due to her calm and polite manner with the patrons. She was meant to be off work for the night, but the head waiter, Tim, had been a no-show again, and as a result Jagriti been asked to cover his evening shift. It meant that this would be her sixth shift in a row, but deep down she didn't care because it got her away from her overbearing parents who were in the process of trying to arrange a marriage for her that she was not remotely interested in. To be fair, it was mainly her father that was pressurising her, but given that her mother never openly challenged her father on her behalf, she felt she had the support of neither parent. Jagriti spent most of her days at university studying to be a nurse and her evenings seemed to increasingly be taken up as a casual waitress at Alessandro's Cucina. She dreaded having no income when her student placement started next year.

Jagriti felt stifled and couldn't quite figure out why. She had loving parents and was on a great career path, but something was missing. Her life had an emptiness to it. She wouldn't describe herself as depressed, but rather if she thought about it, she was *repressed*. Sometimes her father scared her. He was so domineering and it was his way or the highway when it came to any major decision-making. While she understood this was partly a cultural norm, she could not help but feel frustrated when her other Indian friends living in Australia were so much more relaxed and freer to make their own choices. It didn't seem fair. Jagriti had zero interest in Deepak, her supposed love suitor who had been carefully selected by her father. She was pretty sure the poor boy felt the same as she did about the whole thing given that she hadn't sensed any chemistry between them at all. Deepak seemed to avoid eye contact with her so the whole thing was a sham based on her father's idea of the ideal mixed gene pool and academic credentials.

Jagriti dreamed of marrying a blue-eyed Caucasian boy. She had a friend, Jovani, who was half-Indian and half-English, and her mixed genes meant she was blessed with devastatingly good looks. Jovani had dark skin, long black hair and piercing blue eyes. She turned heads wherever she went and made Jagriti feel rather plain. On the rare occasions that Jagriti styled her hair, dressed up and wore make-up, she also received attention, but she always assumed people were merely being polite when they gave her a compliment. In any case, beauty was only skin deep and she believed that who she was as a person was much more important.

Jagriti was always fascinated by the groups of girls who ate at Alessandro's Cucina. It seemed to be in the in place for twenty-first birthdays because of the restaurant's unusual pizza toppings. The typical group would have fake tans, duck lips and eyelashes like a camel. The girls tended to spend most of their night taking pictures of their pizzas or of the group pouting and little time enjoying the ambience and the food. Jagriti wasn't judging; after all she was the odd one out, but somehow she felt old fashioned when she watched them because she simply couldn't relate to the majority of her own generation. Her mother always told her that she had an old head on young shoulders, and she wasn't sure if it was a compliment or an insult.

·· • ● • ··

At 5.57pm, Jacob entered the restaurant to collect the takeaway pasta he'd ordered. If the truth be known, the pasta wasn't actually pasta at all, because the dish was made with zoodles. Jacob had tried numerous times without success to persuade Jackie to make zoodles at home but when she found out it meant using a spiralizer to make strands of zucchini in place of real pasta, she had laughed mercilessly at him, which was her way of showing him she thought he was certifiably insane. Jacob frowned and considered how narrow-minded and behind the times his parents were. It was bloody ridiculous, not to mention embarrassing. He was starting to avoid bringing any of his gym mates home these days but, to his annoyance, they would sometimes just turn up. Apparently they thought his parents were 'a good laugh' despite Jacob vehemently disagreeing with them. One night Jacob had secretly tried to make zoodles himself but the spiralizer became jammed and he'd cut his finger on the blade trying to fix it. It was all too hard and he ended up donating it to his girlfriend, Layla. At least *her* family were a bit more open-minded about making healthier food choices.

When Jagriti went to check on the progress of Jacob's takeaway order with the chef, she noted it was nearly 6.00pm and made the quick calculation in her head regarding the extra pay she would receive for working until 11.00pm that night. It was a pity she didn't have a life and nothing much to spend her money on. Little did she know at this point that covering Tim's shift tonight would change her life forever.

Jagriti sighed inwardly as her eyes discreetly swept over Jacob and she made a quick mental assessment. *If this guy was chocolate, he would eat himself.* Despite his obvious good looks and toned physique, this guy's swagger and arrogant manner did nothing for her at all. It was clear that he fancied himself, which was a major turn-off as far as she was concerned.

Feeling awkward on the inside but presenting with a profession-al manner on the outside, Jagriti greeted the handsome older man who'd entered the restaurant directly behind Jacob. *Now this is a sexy older man if I ever saw one. Pity he is too old for me, probably married, and even if he isn't, I doubt I would be his type. Not that I would ever be allowed to marry a man who isn't Indian despite us living in contemporary times in Australia.*

'Do you have a booking, sir?' Jagriti enquired, a small, shy smile playing on her lips.

'I'm just here to hand in a quote, love,' responded the man. When Jagriti looked confused, he elaborated. 'I'm Paul Townsend, a local electrician. The owner wanted some new down lights put in. I thought I'd give him the costings on my way home rather than by email. I'm old school.' Paul grinned at Jagriti, displaying even white teeth, his green eyes crinkling at the corners. Jagriti noticed how chiselled his stubbled jaw was and how it complimented his square chin. Jagriti guessed Paul was in his late thirties but the truth was he was wearing extremely well for fifty-three years of age. He looked around the dining room as if trying to seek out the manager.

'Ah, I see,' Jagriti said and smiled. 'Alan the manager has already gone for the night, but I can put the quote in the tray in his office if you like?'

Just when Paul was about to agree that Jagriti's suggestion was most helpful and be on his merry way, Farzad entered the restaurant. The atmosphere immediately changed. Paul paused uncertainly mid-speech, due to being troubled by the sudden change in the general vibe. Paul glanced over his shoulder at the odd-looking man behind him and a feeling of unease swept over him. He noted the man had traces of white powder on the tip of his nose and his stomach flip-flopped. This was not a good sign.

It was 6.00pm on the dot. Everything was about to change. Farzad could smell death in the air and knew that the timeline of events would be reported on as commencing at 6.00pm. The journalists loved timelines. He could already see the headline, *Gunman entered at precisely 6.00pm.* He looked around wildly and liked what he saw. His heart was thudding and his eyes were bulging. He was feeling so pumped. *It's on like fucking Donkey Kong. I believe this is where we will finally become the Chosen Seven! Tonight, we will make history!*

CHAPTER 5

Paul had recently separated from his wife, Mandy. Their two sons were now nineteen and twenty-one years old and were both at university interstate. It was the familiar old scenario that often happened when the kids become independent and the couple were left with little to talk about because the children had been their main focus for all those years. The truth was that they had grown apart and often sat in awkward silences over dinner these days.

One night after an especially dull dinner whereby neither of them uttered a single word, Mandy cleared her throat and said in a shaky voice, 'Paul, we need to talk.' Paul glanced up from his plate of spaghetti and stopped mid-twirl of his fork. He knew by her serious, nervous tone that he would probably not like whatever was coming next.

'I, uh, oh God this is not easy.' Mandy covered her face with her hands, and then quickly composed herself. 'I want a divorce, Paul. We are not living our lives to the full, we are merely existing, and I'm just not happy anymore.' A single tear trickled down the left side of Mandy's nose. Paul put his fork down. His appetite had all but disappeared and a tight knot appeared in his stomach.

'Just like that, hey?' he replied in a soft tone, the hurt evident on his face. 'So, there's no discussion or counselling or working through things?' He looked sadly at Mandy. Subconsciously, he had seen it coming, but to hear it out loud was like the proverbial slap in the face.

'Is there someone else?' Paul asked, his eyes suddenly hardening. *Jeez now I'm using clichéd lines.*

'No, of course not!' Mandy was quick to defend herself, but it was not lost on Paul that her cheeks flushed a dull red at the question and she was blinking rapidly the way she did when she wasn't being entirely honest. Paul wanted to believe her because he could only deal with one painful emotion at a time – for now it was hurt and if there was betrayal too… well, that would have to wait for another day.

'Look I know things have soured between us lately, we hang out less and we haven't exactly been active in the bedroom, but isn't this all par for the course as we get older? Do we seriously just throw in the towel after twenty-five years?' Paul's voice began to rise considerably.

Mandy's voice trembled as she answered. 'I will always care about you, Paul, but it's over and has been for a while. I love you but am not *in* love with you. I'm moving in with my mum next week and then we can talk about what happens with the house and the money side of things. I think we need to think about telling the boys and try to stay amicable for their sake.' Mandy knew she was talking too fast, trying to get the worst of the conversation over and done with. No matter what Paul suggested, she was not open to it, and so just like that, their marriage was over.

Mandy promptly moved in with her mother and left Paul in the family home. They decided to keep the home until such time that their sons would no longer be coming home for the university holidays. Hopefully both boys would find post-study work and be able to afford to move out sooner rather than later. Only then would they sell the family home and split their assets.

Paul was a reasonable man with a mature outlook. He tried to take the separation on the chin, but in reality he was gutted. It was hard to accept such a huge life change despite his pragmatic approach. He had a few close friends that he could lament with over a beer or two, but he was seriously struggling to fight the black feelings that threatened to engulf him at times. He threw himself into work, and thankfully due to his reliability, fair prices and admirable work ethics, his business, Townsend Electrical Services, continued going from strength to strength. Paul seemed completely oblivious to the fact that at fifty-three, he was still an extremely handsome and sexy man. He was fit and toned and with his salt-and-pepper hair, crinkly green eyes and chiselled jaw, women checked him out constantly. Paul had never been the type to chase after women and he rarely noticed the signs when they blatantly flirted with him. He had been a loyal and dependable husband and not one of Mandy's friends could figure out for the life of them why she had let him go. A couple of her single friends had their sights set on him but felt it was too soon to make a move. It would also spell the end of their friendship with Mandy so it was too complicated to think about going there.

Following the separation, one of Mandy's so-called friends, Janet, decided to invent an electrical job and claimed she desperately needed it done. When she rang Paul using her best breathy Marilyn Monroe voice, he had scratched his head in bewilderment at the other end of the line. Following Janet's explanation that she needed more power points in her bedroom, he couldn't fathom out why because he'd already put extra ones in for her a couple of years ago. All the same, Paul went around to her house to figure out if it was feasible to undertake the work. He was completely oblivious to the fact that Janet seemed to have just stepped out of the shower and had nothing on but a rather short blue silk kimono. Avoiding her intense gaze, he'd told Janet there was maybe room for one more power point, quoted a rough cost and then stood up to leave. Janet let her robe fall open a little and displayed a dangerous amount of cleavage. She had a lustful look in her eyes as she tried desperately to lure Paul into her arms by presenting with an irresistible sexual aura. Unfortunately, he didn't take the hint and Janet was left muttering obscenities under her breath when he left. She stood with her arms folded looking out her bedroom window as he drove off after handing her an estimate. *What a stupid prick! I was basically handing it to him on a plate!* Feeling rather unsatisfied, Janet threw off her kimono and serviced herself with her giant rabbit vibrator instead. She thought about waiting for her husband Eric to get home, but quite frankly, the thought of his fat gut heaving around on top of her was not floating her boat. *Hmph! At least I'm guaranteed an orgasm with my dildo! So much for that book I paid $40 for that claims reading it guarantees you will become an irresistible temptress! Paul is probably a shit shag anyway! There must be some valid reason that Mandy left him after all…*

Ironically, as Paul sat feeling lonely most nights, there were several women fantasising about what they would like to do to him. As Paul suspected, Mandy was not being entirely truthful about there being no one else, at least in the mental rather than physical sense. She worked in an office in the city and had been flirting with an Italian barista named Tony for months now. Tony's family owned the café that Mandy frequented every day on her lunch break. It was a well-known fact that Tony's father Mario asked his handsome son to stay at the front of house as the main barista. Tony knew the women were crazy for him. He was irresistible, with twenty-five-year-old smooth olive skin, huge chocolate-brown eyes and slicked black hair. He liked to bat his baby browns at the women and as a result they bought coffee in droves. Not only was he eye candy for all the cougars, he was a charmer too. Tony knew how to keep the ladies coming and he didn't just mean back to order more coffee…

Mandy just happened to be going through a mid-life crisis and wanted to prove to herself that she still 'had it', whatever 'it' was. At forty-eight years old, Mandy was still attractive, with shoulder-length light brown hair, almond-shaped hazel eyes and curves in all the right places. She currently felt like a bored old hag. There had been no excitement between her and Paul for some time and she'd started to take him for granted. When her sons became independent, she suddenly felt the urge to live life to the full and 'find herself' again. Her roles as a wife and mother had consumed her for so long that she couldn't quite remember what it was like to focus entirely on herself. Mandy often fantasised about running away to start a new life. She wanted to travel and be carefree and… shock, horror… she wanted to have sex with someone other than Paul. After fantasising about Tony for some time,

Mandy became fixated with the younger man and started making a little more effort with her work attire and make-up.

Mandy started showing a little more leg here and there, followed by some cleavage, and when her bunions weren't playing up, she would wear her sky-high black patent heels. It was not lost on Tony, who found it all rather amusing. If he had a dollar for every woman who thought he only flirted with them exclusively, well he would be rich enough to open his own freakin' café. Tony played the part well and was a master at making women think they were unique and special. He would hold their gaze a little longer, brush their hands against his when giving them their change and give them a jaunty little intimate wink. It was all a big game to him and he loved it.

The game got out of hand when Tony's cousin Joe joined the family business. Joe was a waiter and as much of a charmer as Tony. As Tony and Joe were close in age, they were equally full of testosterone and both had the urge to have sex as often as possible. They were cocky and arrogant so it wasn't long before a battle of the egos ensued. One night after they knocked off and locked up the café, they sat chatting over a few beers. They added up all the regular female customers they reckoned they could easily get into bed at the snap of their fingers. Rather than prove they could bed every one of them, they narrowed it down to three criteria for their unsuspecting prey.

Tony scratched his crotch thoughtfully as he considered what the criteria should be. 'Okay, let's narrow it down to a novelty shag, a rich shag and an old shag. That bird who is the basketballer and twice my height and build – Joanne, I think her name is?' Joe nodded to indicate he knew the customer Tony meant. 'Yep, well she is gonna be my novelty shag as it will be like rooting a bird on stilts!' Both men burst out laughing before Tony continued, 'So for the rich one, I was thinking of that posh bird with the Mercedes and the Gucci handbag collection. She's kinda short and dumpy. Her name is Karen or Kerry or some shit?' Joe nodded once again to confirm he knew the customer. Tony scratched his chin with a hairy hand, his face screwed up with concentration. 'Okay, for the old one, hmm let me think,' he said. Tony's dark fringed lashes cast a shadow on his face.

He looked down as if focusing on a crumb on the table would give him inspiration. 'Got it!' he fist-pumped the air triumphantly. 'That Mandy bird! Old enough to be my mum! Okay looking but tits and ass are sagging a bit – whatcha reckon?'

The two men burst into peals of dirty laughter and Joe whacked the table with his hand in glee. It was his turn to think up three unsuspecting female prey. The men continued on with their disrespectful conversation about their female customers and by the end of the evening, a bet was on to see who could bed all three of their choices first. Of course there was no way of proving their achievements, but each trusted the other would not lie. They did have some integrity, apparently.

CHAPTER 6

Six months ago

Regina sashayed down Fifth Avenue, her dark, beady eyes taking in all the elaborate window displays. She loved her place of birth and was proud to be a New Yorker, but she knew she was no Ms Fancy Pants and would never be that lady who shopped at Saks for designer wares. Regina was proud of her upbringing in the Bronx, and while she had done well for herself and now earned a decent salary, somehow, she couldn't bring herself to spend it on fancy schmnancy clothes, bags and shoes like her colleagues. Having been brought up by a mother who lived on welfare payments (which mainly paid for her drug habit), Regina learned pretty quickly that if she got her hands on any money, she had to spend it wisely and save what she could in order to get by. It was a hard habit to break after she had taken on the responsibility of bringing up her baby brother Zion. Regina did have a weakness for make-up though, and occasionally, she would treat herself to a new lip gloss from the expansive, world-famous make-up store Sephora. Regina justified this as she felt her generous lips were her best feature and deserved to be shown off in the most flattering way. She would never admit it to anyone, but she had a collection of over fifty luscious lip glosses in various shades. Sometimes it felt too indulgent when she thought of those in her old neighbourhood doing it tough, but she would always justify it by exclaiming to the staff in Sephora, 'Don't I deserve to look mighty fine?'

Of course, they would nod and smile regardless of their opinion, because no one would mess with Regina.

Regina was on her way to her fortnightly lunch date with Zion. They both worked centrally; otherwise neither of them would be seen dead in such a poser's paradise. Zion was the head chef at a fancy eatery only three blocks from Regina's office. While he possessed reasonable culinary skills, he had only landed this plum job due to Regina threatening to expose the extremely rich owner for some dodgy business transactions she was privy to if he didn't instantly promote her brother. Zion had no idea this was why he had quickly risen to the rank of head chef and believed it was due to his own talents. This pleased Regina to no end as her baby brother had always lacked self-confidence. It was amazing what believing in yourself could achieve. Now that he thought he was top chef material, he was genuinely motivated and producing some great dishes. Before long, he would have earned the title for real. Regina smiled as she thought fondly of Zion. They were close-knit siblings and always would be.

Regina was almost at her destination when she saw a well-dressed young couple arguing across the street. The man was sneering at the woman and talking to her in a condescending manner. Regina stopped and stared while everyone else scurried past with their eyes averted. Regina's eyes narrowed and her nostrils flared in anger as she looked on. The man appeared to not like the woman's answer to his comment, and he shoved her roughly from behind, causing her to lose her balance and twist her ankle as she stumbled forward. Embarrassed, the woman gave a furtive glance around her, hoping that no one had seen her partner of one year treat her this way.

The couple were caught up in the moment, oblivious to Regina watching the whole exchange with her hands on her hips, a furious scowl on her face. Regina was not in earshot but could see the woman's face crumple as she began to cry.

'Not on my fucking watch!' barked Regina at the top of her voice. Two men in suits walked by and glanced at each other as if to say 'nutter alert'. Regina could not give a rat's ass if people thought she was nuts, she was furious! She

trotted as fast as she could to catch up with the couple, her large bosom heaving with exertion. 'Hey, you!' she shrieked at the man, who was attempting to walk self-righteously back to his office post-lunch break. The woman who'd started to slump despondently in the other direction stopped in her tracks and turned around, staring fearfully at Regina. New York City was full of crazy people! She honestly didn't need anything to make her partner any angrier than he already was. After all, she was the dumbass for forgetting to do all the errands he'd told her to, so it was her own stupid fault!

Regina reached up and grabbed the man roughly by his collar then swung him around to face her. 'What the fu…' he did not get the full sentence out before Regina punched him square on the nose.

'Ain't no muthafucka gonna mess with a lady in front of my crazy ass!' she shrieked at him. Embarrassed and not feeling so tough now, the man cowered and staggered backwards to get away from this madwoman. His hand went up to his face. To his horror, he felt blood spurt from his nose and onto his crisp white Armani shirt.

'You crazy bitch!' he hissed, as he desperately raked in his suit pocket for a tissue to stem the blood. He was not about to tackle this heavyset dark-skinned woman, as she looked like she would make mincemeat out of him. People stopped and stared. 'Someone call the cops!' an onlooker yelled.

Regina noted the woman she'd just stuck up for already had her phone in her hand. 'Are you seriously callin' the cops when I just saved your dumb ass?' Regina barked in the woman's face. The woman looked down at her phone, then back up at Regina, clearly conflicted. Regina pointed a stubby red-nailed finger in her face. 'You need to learn to stand up for yourself and get the fuck away from that asshole! Is that how y'all wanna be treated your whole life? Like some dumb piece of shit? I did you a favour, lady, and don't you forget it!' Regina spat in the man's direction, who jumped backwards to miss being sprayed, a horrified expression on his face. Regina stormed off down the street, muttering obscenities. She needed to disappear out of sight before the cops arrived on the scene. She knew none of the bystanders would come after her or try and take her on. Regina was well aware that she was a force to be reckoned with and she used it to her advantage.

By the time Regina met up with Zion, she'd calmed down somewhat. When she hugged her brother to greet him, he exclaimed, 'Sis, is that blood on your knuckles?' he shook his head in wonderment and guessed accurately that she'd just stepped in to manage an unjust situation. That was how she rolled.

'Sure is!' retorted Regina, puffing her chest out proudly. 'You know me! I ain't gonna stand back and watch no dude messin' with his chick!' Zion laughed heartily, sorry he'd missed the drama. He loved watching Regina in action. No one ever dared mess with his big sister and it always made him feel safe and proud.

Unfortunately, Brian Lipton, the director of the company Regina worked for, had walked out of a shop nearby and witnessed Regina's attack on the unsuspecting man earlier. He did not know the context behind her attack but even if he did, he could not justify an employee behaving like this. Regina was out of control and quite frankly, while he trusted the company manager, Peter Jones, to hire and fire staff, he'd always had reservations about him hiring Regina due to her fiery and abrasive nature. Brian could not deny, however, that she was a damned good software and applications programmer. Her skills seemed in direct contrast to her background and upbringing. On the one hand, Brian admired that Regina had come from nothing to end up in such a good position, but on the other hand, the snobby part of him thought, 'you can take the girl out the Bronx, but you can't take the Bronx out of the girl'. Shaking his head, he speed-dialled Peter to discuss how the incident should be managed.

When Regina returned to the office later that afternoon after making Zion cry with laughter at her latest antics, she was called in to see her boss. Peter had given Brian's call some thought and did not want to take disciplinary action against Regina despite the strict company policy on employee conduct. She was great at her job, and he was more than a little intimidated by her. He'd winced when Brian told him she was out of control and punched a man square on the nose in the middle of Fifth Avenue. He was not keen to be her next victim.

Only last week, the leadership team had gathered to discuss who may be a good candidate to be put forward for the opportunity to spend a year in Australia to gain work experience. The skills of their employees were in demand in Australia and visas would not be difficult to obtain. A few names were discussed but no definitive outcome was reached. Now Peter saw this as the solution to the problem. He would offer the opportunity to Regina but not before giving her a massive lecture on how she was expected to behave when representing the company overseas.

CHAPTER 7

Friday 17 May 2019, 6.01pm

Farzad whipped out his sawn-off shotgun so quickly that Jagriti's brain could not seem to register what her eyes were seeing. The word 'oh' gargled out of her throat but her lips remained as though they had frozen in time while uttering this.

Paul was quicker to react. 'What the fuck?' he instinctively took a step back, his eyes narrowed and his shoulders squared, while he tried to stand protectively in front of Jagriti.

'EVERYBODY WILL FUCKING LISTEN TO ME RIGHT NOW,' screamed Farzad at the top of his lungs. His eyes were bulging and a huge vein was throbbing on the left side of his neck. He bobbed around nervously on the balls of his feet like a sportsman warming up, his tall bulky frame making him appear awkward. The murmur of background chatter between customers stopped abruptly. The tinkling noise of plates and cutlery also ceased. Suddenly there was a deadly silence, an ominous chill in the air, and all eyes were on Farzad. He pulled himself up to his full height with his chest puffed out. He was sweating profusely and it was making him irritable. He pushed his black curls out of his eyes and his glasses back up his nose before sweeping his free hand through his greasy hair. *I've waited a long time for this.*

I can't fuck it up now. Don't spoil the fun before it has begun. Be patient and the best outcome will be achieved. Focus, focus, focus.

When the staff and patrons began to realise they were at the mercy of a madman, different responses ensued. This was exactly what Farzad wanted. He had everyone's full attention now. The staff looked like stone statues as they ground to a halt, rooted to their individual spots. The chefs at the servery stood dead still, one of them with a serving spoon still in his hand. He held it in mid-air with peas in it, not daring to put them down on the plate in front of him.

A waiter stood at a table with a bottle of champagne in his hand that he was about to pour for a couple having high tea to celebrate their twenty-fifth wedding anniversary. He too was rooted to the spot, too afraid to move. The woman at the table began to sob. 'SHUT THE FUCK UP!' Farzad screamed at the woman, who was becoming hysterical. The woman merely cried harder. Her husband managed to discreetly call triple zero on his mobile phone, which was hidden on his lap. He dared not speak but prayed that the operator could hear what was going on in the background and pick up on the location so they could send help. The man's heart hammered painfully in his chest while adrenaline began to flood his body.

Farzad lowered his voice a few octaves in an attempt to sound sinister. He spoke evenly and slowly. 'I'm gonna make an example of people who piss me off, so you better listen good! I want everyone to put their mobile phones and wallets in this breadbasket.' Farzad waved the gun at the breadbasket on the nearest table. 'Then I want all of you to sit down on the floor in front of me where I can see you. Come up one by one with your stuff. Once you drop it in the basket, you sit the fuck down and keep quiet. Get over here right now!' His voice rose again as he pointed the gun briefly down at the floor to indicate where his captives were to assemble.

As the hostages made their way gingerly to the breadbasket to deposit their items then head down to the floor, a few more stifled sobs and wails of despair could be heard.

Farzad became aware that more than one person was crying now. He hated cry-babies, so they better shut the hell up before he shut them up permanently. The sea of solemn faces and trembling limbs was giving him a real boner and he hoped no one had noticed.

'I want silence! No fucking crying or carrying on! No talking and no questions until I say so!' Farzad roared at his captors. His bulbous eyes continued to scan the room, a protruding vein throbbing at his temple. Farzad had in his mind that there could only be seven people including him. His superstitious streak meant he felt the need to use his lucky number. It was a small enough number of people to manage, but at the same time, it was enough people to make an impact on the lives of those who cared about them. The rest of the world would watch on. It would be glorious.

The sobbing woman was unable to compose herself and her husband grew increasingly anxious. He badly wanted to say some words of comfort to his wife but was afraid to break the rules by talking. Farzad was noting everyone's demeanour, relishing every moment, seeking out the chosen ones. He looked down at Jagriti, who sat directly in front of him. She looked calm and her expression was impassive, her expression giving nothing away. He liked that about her. If he couldn't read her thoughts, then that made her special and she could well be an asset to him. Farzad pointed the gun at her. 'You! Get up now! Stand beside me!' Trembling on the inside but stoic on the outside, Jagriti stood up obediently, her expression blank. Farzad noted the middle-aged man beside her flinch. His eyes hardened and his jaw tightened. The man was obviously protective of women. That could be fun.

'You!' Farzad's eyes met Paul's. 'Join your little friend over here.' Reluctantly, Paul stood up, his eyes boring defiantly into Farzad's as he joined Jagriti, his mind racing. *Is this guy a terrorist? Is his bark worse than his bite? I need to establish exactly what he wants so we can get out of here alive. First, he tells us to sit and now he tells us to stand; his thinking is erratic…*

The woman continued to sob loudly. Farzad was not impressed at her constant distraction during the special moments of picking the chosen ones. He marched over to her and told her to lie face down on the floor. No one dared move a muscle or look in her direction. Her husband shook uncontrollably and strange gasping noises began to escape from his lips. The woman trembled as she lay face down on the floor as requested, her head slightly raised. 'Please don't shoot me, we have kids and a grandson on the way!' she sobbed into the patterned tiles. Although her comment was muffled, Farzad registered what she said and it infuriated him. *Why the fuck do people think it makes them special because they have offspring? Is my life less worthy because I walk the Earth alone?*

Farzad made a snap decision. 'COCKSUCKER!' he screamed, as he shot her square in the back. The almighty bang reverberated around the room and shook the very foundations of the restaurant as her body instantly slumped forward.

Levi began to scream a loud guttural animalistic sound that she did not recognise. It was like she was listening to someone else and experiencing an out-of-body experience. It overpowered the mayhem of the other hostages crying, swearing and lamenting.

'BASTARD!' screamed Regina, her face contorted with fury, her fists curled.

Farzad fired his gun up towards the roof to get everyone's attention. 'SILENCE!' he roared as the bullet ricocheted off the ceiling and hit the floor.

A horrified hush descended over Alessandro's Cucina. Everyone was trying their best to stay composed. No one wanted to suffer the same fate as the poor woman who lay shot and bleeding before them. With hammering hearts and terror rushing through their veins, the captives were all silently praying to be spared their lives. The victim died almost instantly. Thankfully, her head was facing away from her husband, who was spared from seeing the life ebb away from her. Farzad was fascinated by his handiwork. Her staring, soulless eyes and the blood bubbling from her mouth was just like how it was in the movies. He realised he was getting off on it and suddenly understood how murder could become an addiction.

The hostages were completely sickened by the fact that the gunman would not let anyone attend to the woman who had been shot. Given that he'd threatened to blow everyone away if the police or paramedics came near the restaurant, there was little anyone could do about it.

Jagriti witnessed the excruciating look of loss and pain on the face of the woman's husband. He was wracked with silent tears that made his entire body convulse. It was so tragic that this couple were here to celebrate one of life's joyful moments only to suffer needlessly at the hands of a madman. She knew it was a harrowing moment she would never forget – if she lived to tell the tale. The thought that she may not get out of this alive was one that she could not allow to consume her. Jagriti had strong survival instincts and she intended to use them. Jagriti was well attuned to her attributes and her ability to help others. This was why she studied nursing even though she harboured a secret desire to become a world-famous Indian chef. She tried to be her usual pragmatic self but still let out a barely audible gulp while she attempted to feign a look of bravado that she simply did not feel.

Farzad noted that when he had given out his initial instructions, the large dark-skinned lady who sat at the far-right hand corner did not rush to obey his orders. She had serious attitude. He could tell just by assessing her body language. Her expression was one of outrage, her nostrils were flared and she looked like she was weighing up taking him on. He thought she may turn out to be entertaining. 'You!' he jerked his head in her direction. 'Join these two!' he nodded at Jagriti and Paul. Farzad had never felt so powerful. This was the biggest high he had experienced in all of his forty-five years. Cocaine, orgies and erotic asphyxiation did not come close. That was for little boys, not a real man like him. Impulsively, Farzad yelled, 'All the staff get out now! Quick before I change my motherfuck-ing mind! Go and spread the word, I want you to make sure the world is watching and listening!' The relief etched on the faces of the chefs and wait staff was palpable.

Instinctively, Jagriti knew the offer to leave did not extend to her and she was proven to be correct. After the remaining staff left in a dazed and shocked state, Farzad demanded that Jagriti lock the main door of the restaurant and place the keys in the designated breadbasket. As Jagriti obediently followed his orders, she noted the pallor of the man who had just lost his wife. He had gone into shock. His skin was clammy and grey. The poor man looked like he had mentally checked out. It was the most heartbreaking scene Jagriti had ever witnessed.

CHAPTER 8

Three weeks ago

It was a rainy Saturday morning and Jacob was in between clients at the local gym. He'd completed two early morning personal training sessions already and just stopped to drink a protein shake to refuel his tired muscles. He thought with pompous satisfaction about all the losers who were still in bed after partying last night. His old school mates had invited him to some chick's twenty-first birthday party but he knew they would pressure him to drink beer and he'd already counted out his exact micronutrients and macronutrients for the week, and beer did not factor into it. His body was a temple, after all. Jacob was mainly strict with his diet but occasionally allowed himself to eat whatever he wanted for dinner; otherwise it became unsustainable. Even then, his cheat meal would be a small portion. Jacob had slowly brought his mum around to making a few high-protein, low-carbohydrate meals now and then, much to the utter disgust of his dad. Jacob pulled a few poses in the mirror whilst flexing his biceps and asked his fellow gym instructor Sam to take some photos so he could update his Instagram page. Almost instantly Jacob's Instagram news feed was flooded with 'likes' and comments about how 'ripped' he was. Feeling satisfied, his ego well and truly boosted, he looked out for his next client, Sue, who just happened to be his mum's friend and the mum of his sister's best friend.

Sue annoyed Jacob a little. She did not seem to take her sessions seriously enough and as a result she wasn't getting the best outcomes with weight loss and toning that she should be. Jacob didn't care about the effect this had on Sue but he did care about it not being a good look for business. He prided himself on those before and after pictures of his clients so he could brag on his blog about them.

Sue was running late for her personal training session with Jacob because she was hungover. Jackie was to blame. Jacob knew this because he'd just received a text message from Sue that read, 'Sorry! Running a few minutes late – lucky I managed to get out of bed at all after being out on the sauce with your mum last night ha ha! See you soon!'

Jacob sighed in exasperation. His mum seriously needed to grow up and start acting her age. When Jackie and Sue went out together, they managed to revert back to behaving like teenagers. It annoyed their respective husbands so much that they'd stopped going out as couples. This suited Jackie and Sue just fine and meant that they could ramp up their antics and bring out their wild side as much as they pleased. Last night had been no exception.

It started out innocently enough with the two women meeting in a pizzeria with the intention of having dinner and a couple of glasses of wine. The problem was that the pizzeria had $8 cocktails on Fridays – so cheap and too damn delicious and refreshing. After several cosmopolitans and margaritas, they'd gone on to a lively pub with a cool DJ that was mainly frequented by patrons half their age. 'Let's show them how's its done,' shrieked Jackie with glee and she started shimmying to the song 'Dirrty' by Christina Aguilera. The fact that the DJ was dedicating the night to playing music from the early 2000s was definitely a contributing factor to Jackie and Sue not calling it a night when they should have. Sue joined in by doing a rather risqué 'slut drop' dance move and the two women began crying with laughter at how hilarious and entertaining they were. Due to being instantly transported back to almost twenty years ago by the song, their subconscious memories took them back to another era and they both began shrieking out of tune along with the music belting out of the speakers. Looking over at a group of bewildered onlookers, Jackie thrust out her hips, looked straight at them and sang at the top of her voice, 'Want to get dirty, it's about time that I came to start the party, sweat dripping over my body!'

Jacob's girlfriend, Layla, was there with her friends at the other side of the bar. Jackie was too drunk to notice her son's girlfriend watching her with a mixture of admiration and horror. Layla nudged her friend Georgia and yelled over the music, 'That's Jacob's mum and her friend – check out the state of them!'

Georgia's eyes rounded as she watched the two older women dancing with wild abandon, and she started laughing. 'Oh my God, they are kinda cool, like they don't give a shit what anyone thinks of them!'

Layla nodded. 'I know, Jacob would be mortified if he was here though, ha ha! I'm not sure whether to mention it to him or not.'

'Which one is his mum?' Georgia peered at them more closely.

Layla clapped a hand over her mouth. 'Oh my God! It's the one that's just started dirty dancing with Peter Lynch, who used to be in my home group at school! That's it! I'm not telling Jacob! He will go nuts! I'm off to Europe next week anyhow so won't see him or his crazy family for a couple of months!' Giggling, the two girls moved further away from the older women and their antics. If Layla wanted to avoid dropping Jackie in it for embarrassing herself then she'd better lay low and make sure their paths didn't cross tonight. There was little chance of Jackie noticing her, though, as she had double vision at this point and wasn't convinced it was just the dirty dancing making the room spin…

· • ● • ·

Jackie and Sue could barely remember walking along a residential street in their mutual suburb on the way home. However, the one thing that stood out in their minds was when Jackie fell backwards over someone's front garden hedge and lay laughing helplessly on the lawn. Sue hissed frantically at her from the street, 'Quick, get up before the owner comes out,' but when she leaned forward to reach out and help Jackie up, she also lost her balance and toppled over the hedge, promptly face planting onto the grass. At this point Jackie felt a bit of pee come out as she tried hard to control her bodily functions. Both women were hysterical and clutching their stomachs because they ached so much from laughing while they rocked with mirth on some stranger's lawn.

Eventually, the porch lights came on and an elderly white-haired man came out, dressed in blue and white striped flannelette pyjamas and brown velvet slippers. He was furious and pointed his walking cane at them threateningly. 'Off my property now, you disgusting creatures, or I'm phoning the police.' The two women looked at each other as they lay side by side on the grass and while both fully intended to be respectful and apologise, instead they burst into fresh shrieks of uncontrollable laughter. Sue honestly thought her stomach muscles were going to give up on her, they hurt so much.

The old man walked slowly over to them, his bandy legs making him unsteady as he approached. He tapped the tip of his walking cane on Jackie's shoulder and yelled, 'SHOO!' Jackie's response to being talked to as though she was a dog was to rock silently with silent laughter like she had been winded. Somehow she managed to wet her pants in the process. Jackie willed herself to scramble to her feet. She was soaking wet from the dew on the grass and from pee. She knew she should be horrified and ashamed of herself but it was simply the best fun she'd had in ages. The old man stood staring at them, his hooded eyes never leaving them until they'd staggered down the front path, unlatched the gate and disappeared from sight. Once he was satisfied that the two revolting harlots were far enough away from his property for him to return inside, he tried ringing his son Bill to offload about his feral trespassers. He could simply not understand why his son never returned his calls. He'd rung Bill at least ten times this month and the selfish bastard never called him back. The old man surmised that his son would probably end up old and lonely just like him due to his inability to maintain relationships. It did not occur to him for one second that his son was repeating a familial pattern that he himself had role modelled. When he was a child, Bill always seemed puzzled about why his dad never returned his grandad's calls. History was merely repeating itself. Hopping back into bed, he fell into a disgruntled sleep. Those loose women had unnerved him with their free spirits and drunken laughing. What was the world coming to? The old man would never learn of the coincidence that *his son would end up being a hostage alongside the son of the lady he'd just prodded with his cane.*

· · • ● • · ·

Both women knew they would regret overindulging when their duties as wife and mother resumed the following day. When Sue woke up feeling groggy and disorientated, she realised with disdain that she had to go to her stupid personal training session with Jacob that morning because she'd lost a bet the last time she was out with Jackie. Two months ago, Jackie had bet Sue that she wouldn't be able to get the cost of the wine taken off the bill by complaining that her meal wasn't cooked properly. It was a trick they'd used before to reduce the cost of their meals and sometimes it worked and sometimes it didn't. Sue didn't like doing it unless the meal was genuinely mediocre because it was more than a little dishonest, but Jackie was so damn persuasive. On this occasion, it was clear there was nothing wrong with Sue's dish and the restaurant manager quite rightly refused to take the cost of the wine off the bill.

If Sue was unsuccessful in achieving the bill reduction, her penalty was to sign up for six personal training sessions with Jacob. This was a win-win for Jackie as her son was always complaining that his mum didn't try hard enough to get him clients. Sue was completely spewing. She must have been mad and extremely intoxicated to agree to paying such a cruel price for losing a bet. Sue hated working out. After all, it involved lunges, squats and other hideous exercises. But a bet was a bet, and she would have to keep to her side of the bargain as agreed.

Sue was distracted as she drove to the gym. She suspected she probably shouldn't be driving after a big night of drinking, and she was grateful it was only a short journey from her home. She was eight minutes late when she arrived and Jacob looked mighty pissed off. He was going to torture her, she just knew it. Still, she hadn't vomited and managed to get herself there so it was kudos to her as far as she was concerned. Meanwhile, Jackie was at home standing at the kitchen sink, glugging down copious amounts of water. Colin eyed her suspiciously. 'Drunk again, were we?' he tutted his disapproval.

'Leave me alone', muttered Jackie. She pointed at the large glass of water she'd just refilled. 'I'm not in the mood Colin, my mouth is as dry as a nun's crotch.'

Colin looked at her with disgust. 'You are atrocious sometimes, Jackie,' he said and rolled his eyes reproachfully.

Jackie waved a dismissive hand as he left the room. 'Oh well, you know what you can do if you don't like it,' she cackled.

'I heard that!' Colin shot back.

'You were meant to!' she retorted. It was all banter as Colin and Jackie secretly enjoyed their childish back-and-forth fights. It was a bit of a game to see who would back down first. Sometimes they could tell that it shocked their friends, and it did occur to Jackie at times that it wasn't great role modelling to Jacob and Leonie, but surely the kids knew their parents loved each other deep down? Did anyone have a relationship where their partner didn't get on their tits after a few years? Surely not! Jackie shrugged her shoulders. Who was a perfect parent? Adulting was seriously overrated. It didn't get any easier just because you became hideously old and were suddenly expected to display a certain level of maturity and wisdom.

Jackie stared thoughtfully into space. She was still a few years off being fifty so maybe she would grow up then. Or maybe not!

Her thoughts were broken by Colin calling out from the laundry. 'That bloody cat must have pissed on the floor again, it reeks of pee in here!' Suddenly remembering that she'd stripped her clothes off last night and left them on the laundry floor, Jackie dissolved info fits of laughter. Her knees buckled and she clutched the kitchen bench top to stop herself from collapsing in a heap.

It was all coming back to her! Last night she had wet herself from laughing hysterically whilst lying on an old man's lawn! Oblivious to what the hell she was laughing at, Colin merely shook his head and went out to his man shed in the back yard. He was always in there banging and clanging. Sometimes he made impressive things in his workshop and other times he sat drinking beer while watching sports on TV. He wasn't feeling inclined to make anything presently because Jackie had laughed at his homemade shelves a few weeks ago. He still felt *rather sulky about it. So they weren't perfectly straight, so what? Weren't whacky things all the rage when it came to home décor now? Ok so maybe the shelf had collapsed after a heavy vase was placed on it, but he had warned Jackie, who never bloody listened, that it was for light things like trinkets only. Jackie had reminded him she hated trinkets and asked if he'd lost his mind. They had consequently ended up bickering. Needless to say, his lovingly crafted shelf had been taken down and he was left licking his wounds about another DIY project gone wrong. Jackie could be a real bloody pain in the ass at times, but she was still his girl and always would be.*

CHAPTER 9

Friday 17 May 2019, 6.10pm

Regina was fizzing mad. She'd seen her date approach the restaurant through the floor-length glass windows. He'd taken one look at the gunman, his eyes rounded in horror, then taken off, practically running down the street, leaving her infuriated. He was certainly no knight in shining armour. *Fucking pussy! Did he bother to call the cops? If so, where the hell are they? The emergency response times were pathetic in Australia compared with New York!* If the lunatic didn't have a gun, Regina would have taken him on by herself for sure. She was desperate to dig her talon-like nails right into his stupid fat face and tear it to shreds.

Regina took her time joining Jagriti and Paul. She chewed gum casually and sauntered over as though completely unperturbed by the situation. Regina stood with her hands on her ample hips, one foot pointing forward in a defiant stance. She had no intention of being at the mercy of this moron. She just had to work out a plan of action to disarm him. *If I can't control what's happening, I can control how I respond, and that's where the power is. I'm gonna find a way to bust his sorry ass!*

It was now 6.10pm and Farzad was feeling extremely put out by the fact that the emergency services were yet to arrive to negotiate with him. He considered that he had everyone's phone, which would have diminished the chances of anyone calling the police, but by the same token, there were some terrified witnesses who had been set free as well as those who had bolted in the other direction when they saw what was going on through the large glass windows at the front of the restaurant. Surely there should be an army of cops and media out there by now?

Farzad kept reminding himself not to be impulsive, but his unpredictable nature meant that he would often act or talk before his brain had registered what the hell he was doing. He believed this was down to supreme intelligence. *How else do I explain that I am too fast even for my own mind? I am a higher power, a greater man, a divine being of God!*

Farzad looked over at Jacob and determined that he was a mere boy who thought he was a man. All muscles and no life experience. It was obvious! He needed to be taught by none other than the master himself. 'You!' he shook the gun in Jacob's direction. 'Join the others that are standing over there, meathead!' Jacob's eyes were darting around the room. He was desperately looking for a way to escape. *I have to outsmart this psycho, but how?* Realising that he had no option but to obey at this present moment, Jacob slowly rose and joined the others who were standing. He was dismayed to note that he was visibly shaking. He didn't feel at all manly at the moment.

'Are you screwing her?' Farzad was now staring directly at Bill and jerked his head in Levi's direction to indicate he was referring to her. Levi looked utterly disgusted and cast her eyes downwards at the question, but Bill smirked at Farzad with a smug expression, trying to emit a man-to-man look that equated to nudge, nudge, wink, wink and was code for 'not yet mate, but it is my intention'.

Ironically, although Farzad was equally revolting in the way he treated women, he was hypocritical enough to take an instant dislike towards Bill, it being plainly obvious to him that Levi was with him against her will.

'Both of you over there, now!' Farzad jerked his head towards Bill and Levi to indicate they should join the others who were standing. Reluctantly, they did as they were told and trotted obediently over to the rest of the chosen ones.

Farzad wiped the sweat out of his eyes with the back of his hand and noted the cuff of his sweatshirt sleeve was grimy due to continuously doing this. *Where the fuck are the cops? Should I keep the chosen ones as the only hostages? Or should I have some fun with the remaining stragglers in the restaurant? Focus, focus, focus.* He felt like his mind was racing in a million directions. It was like it constantly played spin the wheel of fortune and wherever the dial stopped was what he would randomly choose to do next.

All of a sudden, the man whose wife had been shot leapt up and lunged at Farzad in a frenzy of rage. He managed to stab him in the shoulder with a steak knife that he'd secretly pocketed from the table he had been sitting at. Farzad screamed in pain and fury and instantly shot the man in the chest at close range. The bang was deafening and the smell of gunfire made Farzad feel omnipotent once more. The man slumped to the ground like a ragdoll, a look of surprise on his face as his life ebbed away. Farzad was sure that his own wound was superficial and not life-threatening despite the blood that was starting to soak his beige sweatshirt. He had managed not to drop his gun, which he was pleased about, but he had been caught off guard and was now injured. It could have been disastrous. Damn that stupid man! *Focus, focus, focus!*

Farzad was positive he could smell the fear in the air and it made him feel so high that he almost passed out from euphoria. Faint whimpers were all that could be heard in the restaurant as the horror of the second cold-blooded murder registered for the remaining captives. There was no doubt in anyone's mind now that Farzad meant business and his capabilities had been well and truly established. Farzad made a snap decision. He pointed at the remaining customers on the floor. 'Out now! There can only be the chosen ones remaining!' Once again, he asked Jagriti to open then lock the door behind those that were permitted to leave. 'No funny business or you know what will happen!' he yelled. The chosen ones exchanged wary glances with each other. Individually, they were such different people, but at that moment their thoughts were eerily similar as their fight or flight responses were kicking in. Each was desperately trying to formulate a plan of action to take this lunatic down and each was wondering what the others could offer in terms of making this happen.

On jelly legs, the last remaining patrons headed out the door, a mixture of relief and horror etched on their faces. Some were able to run into the arms of the police who had finally arrived, and others collapsed in shock a few metres along the street. The police had received the information about the potential siege situation from the call centre as soon as the operator dispatched it to patrols, however, a lack of cars in the area resulted in a slower response time than was required. This was something that would be criticised later in the coroner's court given that a major crisis situation was not prioritised due to a lack of resources.

So far, the only background information police had to work on was taken from CCTV footage, which recorded a sinister looking, tall heavyset male with black curly hair and glasses entering the restaurant at 6.00pm. The female operator at the call centre who connected with the now-deceased man had picked up the hint of a West Asian accent when the gunman spoke. She'd determined from the dialogue between the gunman and the hostages that the captor was armed, dangerous and had fired his gun. Unfortunately, much of the recording was muffled. The man had fiddled nervously with the mobile phone on his lap and unknowingly covered the microphone much of the time. Now the grim task lay ahead to find out who had been shot, whether they were injured or dead and whether the gunman was going to allow them access to the victims.

It appeared so far that the gunman intended to make everything as difficult as possible. The news of the hostage situation had quickly spread like wildfire. Neighbouring businesses, office workers and passers-by looked on with shock when armed police with ballistic vests began to cautiously approach the scene to cordon off the immediate vicinity to members of the public.

Those who were lucky enough to escape Farzad's clutches had already begun giving statements about what had happened thus far and provided detailed accounts from each of their individual perspectives. This assisted in building up a profile of the madman. Journalists and local TV stations clamoured to get the latest updates in the hope of scoring an exclusive story. Social media posts begun in earnest and 'armchair experts' surmised who the captor might be and what his motives were. The pessimists commented that he was definitely a terrorist and the hostages were doomed, while the religious people posted thoughts and prayers and encouraged loved ones of the hostages to be strong.

CHAPTER 10

Friday 17 May 2019, 6.20pm

Levi's husband, Ben, picked up their daughter, Charlie, from the childcare centre she frequented and strapped her carefully into her car seat. He often felt guilty that the little mite spent entire days there. What choice did the majority of working parents have these days? They were damned if their children went to childcare and damned if they didn't. People judged no matter how you tried to parent these days. Ben sighed and turned the key in the ignition to set off on the journey home. He was impatient for Levi to come home and spend some precious family time with them. At this rate, he doubted Charlie would be able to stay awake long enough to have a hug and kiss with her mummy. It niggled Ben that Levi's career seemed to be the first priority in their lives. He wasn't judging, on the contrary, he was supportive, proud and wanted her to do well, but the old fashioned part of him couldn't help but wish she was able to be a stay-at-home mum like his had been.

Ben's thoughts drifted while he sat in peak hour traffic. He glanced in his rear-view mirror. Poor Charlie looked like she was already nodding off and was yet to have dinner and a bath. He smiled at how much she looked like a mini Levi. Ben suddenly jerked as his subconscious alerted him to the local news segment on the radio and he quickly turned up the volume just enough to hear it properly but not so loud that it would rouse Charlie. Ben stiffened as he listened to the serious-sounding female news broadcaster.

Tonight, we have breaking news regarding a hostage situation occurring at Alessandro's Cucina in the central business district in Adelaide. It is understood a gunman currently has six hostages at his mercy, however, he has let some patrons and restaurant staff go free. It has been confirmed that two fatal shootings occurred earlier. It is believed the victims are a man and a woman who were dining together but at this stage, their identities remain unknown. We urge anyone whose loved ones may have been dining in the restaurant to come forward and contact police on…

Ben did not hear the rest of the broadcast, his blood had frozen in his veins upon hearing the words 'the victims are a man and a woman who were dining together'. The words kept replaying in his head while he tried desperately not to panic. His last text from Levi was to let him know she definitely had to go through with the dreaded dinner with her boss, Bill, at Alessandro's Cucina. *It can't be Levi, it can't be Levi, it can't be Levi.*

Ben hoped if he said it over and over enough times that it would be true. A woman in the next lane glanced at Ben as they pulled up at the traffic lights. She hoped he was okay; she couldn't help but notice his face was chalk-white and he had the glazed look of someone in shock. *I hope he hasn't just left the scene of an accident,* she thought scornfully. Feeling self-righteous, the woman allowed Ben to make headway in front of her so she could write down his registration number. The woman had a hunch that the pale-looking man had probably hit another car and not owned up. She envisaged the police thanking her for being so astute as to notice his suspicious-looking demeanour. Not that she was a busybody or one for making assumptions about people based on very little or anything. She would have much worse things to focus on when she discovered her sister and brother-in-law had just been murdered in cold blood.

Ben desperately wanted to pull over to call the police but he realised that he could not handle having that conversation with Charlie present because she was bound to pick up on his anxiety. Cursing the slow-moving traffic as he approached yet another set of red traffic lights, he began chewing frantically on his cuticles like he always did in high-stress situations.

·· • ●• ··

Keerti Ghoshal was making homemade chapatis in her large open plan kitchen when she overheard something on TV about the restaurant where her daughter worked. 'Rahul!' she shouted over to her husband, who sat stiffly in his favourite armchair, his head buried in a newspaper. When he did not answer, her voice rose higher. 'RAHUL! Turn up the news, there is a story about Alessandro's Cucina!'

'So what!' grunted Rahul. He was irritated about being interrupted and assumed that the story was something petty like the chef-of-the-year award or some rubbish like that. His stomach was rumbling due to the wonderful aroma of lentil dahl and lamb Rogan Josh curry coming from the pots simmering on the stove. Rahul was not keen on Keerti becoming distracted from her kitchen duties because it meant he would need to wait even longer to fill his belly. Keerti joined him in the lounge, traces of lentil flour still on her hands and the faint scent of cardamom and cumin on her apron. She prodded her husband's shoulder with a bony finger to ensure she had his full attention. Keerti turned up the sound to hear the news reporter give a similar account to the one Ben just heard on the radio. At this stage the details were scant, but when Rahul realised his only daughter was potentially trapped in a hostage situation, he leapt up and yelled, 'Koee kamabakht raasta nahin!' Jagriti's parents looked at each other in unison, each mirroring the anguished expression of the other. 'I must call the police at once and get Jagriti out of there!' cried Rahul, reaching for his mobile phone. Always one to fear the worst, Keerti fainted on the spot.

CHAPTER 11

Zion Terry was suffering from a particularly bad bout of insomnia. It was 4.35am in New York and he was definitely not well rested and ready to face the day. He was feeling uneasy after hanging up with his sister Regina earlier. He knew she could take care of herself but still hadn't been able to shake off the sense that she wasn't safe in Australia. Zion stretched, yawned and clawed at his crotch. *Some pot might take the edge off.* Zion padded through his tiny apartment to the small kitchenette and deftly rolled, then lit, a joint. He lay on his worn brown sofa and blew smoke rings into the air as he stared pensively at the ceiling. Zion expected to feel the usual chilled out feeling wash over him but something was bugging him and he couldn't quite place what it was.

The truth was that he missed Regina badly. She was fourteen years old when he was born and she had more or less brought him up single-handedly. They grew up in the Bronx with their junkie mother who was too out of it to be a fit parent most of the time. They had no idea who their father was or whether they even shared the same one. Given their age gap, they knew that having the same father was possible but not probable. All the same, they still hung on to the dream that the same man had fathered them both. The siblings fantasised that he was their knight in shining armour who would come and take them away from their deprived life and mentally checked out mother one day. Regina and Zion both looked very much like their mother so it wasn't as though they had inherited any mysterious good looks from their father's side. In their fantasies, their father was incredibly handsome and rich and they enjoyed regaling each other with tales about his qualities and good looks.

Regina was a bad ass and got on a lot of people's nerves, but Zion knew that she had no choice but to have an old head on young shoulders due to the cards that life had dealt them. Zion shook his head and chuckled while he thought back to some of the battles Regina had fought for him in the neighbourhood when they were kids. She would take on anybody that got in the way of her family's happiness. Zion laughed out loud as his mind wandered back to the time a couple of bozos tried to break into their humble little apartment while they slept. Regina was seventeen and Zion was only three years old at the time.

After hearing a floorboard creak in the hallway, Regina bolted upright on her camp bed in the tiny room they shared. She put her finger to her lips and said 'ssshh'. Zion also sat up, confused and sleepy with his thumb in his mouth and eyes like saucers as he watched his sister with fascination. Although it was dark, he could see the moonlight shining on Regina's determined face. Her lips were pursed in fury as her large bosom heaved up and down. Both were sure signs that she was pretty mad and about to explode. She stood up and picked up her dresser stool then marched purposefully out to the hallway. As suspected, two male intruders had broken a window and climbed through it. They were now in the small lounge room stuffing what meagre belongings the Terry family had into a bag. Completely enraged by what she was witnessing, Regina charged at them with all her might and smashed one of them over the head with the stool, knocking him out cold. The second guy squared up to her, and with blazing eyes and her teeth bared, she punched him full force in the face, breaking his nose. He toppled backwards with surprise and like his mate, he also lost consciousness as he hit his head on the sideboard going down. Zion wasn't meant to see any of it, but he had not stayed in their bedroom like she'd requested. Regina was his heroine and he would always feel protected with her by his side. Not surprisingly, their mother slept through the entire event after being wiped out from smoking several cones a few hours before. With brute strength, Regina grabbed the culprits under their shoulders one at a time and dragged them out to the front yard. She did not call the police because that was not how things were done in the Bronx. Instead, she kicked the living daylights out of them whilst they were out cold and left them there to make an example of what happened to anyone who messed with the Terry family.

Zion stood rooted to the spot with bug eyes while his sister wiped the sweat out of her narrowed brown eyes, her chest rising and falling rapidly due to the adrenaline pumping through her body. Finally, she spat on the unconscious men and stood up straight. She tossed back her curls and bellowed, 'Ain't no muthafucka gonna fuck with my family – you got that?' she nodded angrily to an imaginary audience. A curtain twitched across the street. 'Damn straight!' she hollered with her hand cupped close to her mouth. Then she scooped up Zion and tucked him back into bed. His big sister always made him feel safe. Despite the violence he witnessed, he knew from a young age that in order to survive, he needed to adopt an 'it's them or us' mentality.

As his thoughts returned to the present, Zion sat up and decided to check Facebook to see if there were any signs of how Regina's date was going back in Australia. She'd been about to walk out of the restaurant when he'd called her earlier. By calling when he did, he had bought the dude a few more minutes of her precious time. Zion chuckled softly as he imagined her growing impatient. Zion found Regina's Facebook post where she had 'checked in' at Alessandro's Cucina but then there was nothing more, no photos or comments. Then, the intuitive search function on his phone detected the words 'Alessandro's Cucina' and his news feed was suddenly flooded with the breaking news about the siege situation in South Australia. *What the hell?* Zion knew instinctively that Regina would be one of the hostages and did not know whether to laugh or cry. He knew one thing for sure. Regina would *not* go down without a fight. *Holy cow, my sister needs me and I don't know what to do.* Zion sat with his head in his hands, feeling stupid and helpless. If he hadn't rung his sister when he did, she would probably have left the restaurant unscathed. It was all his stupid fault and now he didn't know how to fix it. He was shit at problem-solving. All he could do was believe in Regina. He knew she could get out of this. After all, no one had gotten the better of her up to now, so why should this situation be any different? Although he was trying to think reassuring and positive thoughts, Zion's stomach was tight with fear. He tried to focus solely on the belief Regina was invincible to convince himself that she would survive.

Zion suddenly felt suffocated in his tiny apartment and decided to walk the few blocks to Central Park in a bid to get his head straight about his next move. He heard that the New York Police Department (NYPD) issued tickets to anyone who entered the park between 1.00am and 6.00am but he didn't believe it. After all, how would you issue the homeless and the addicts with tickets if police can't rouse them? Supposing they could be roused, would they be able to afford to pay the fines? It was an absolute joke. Zion decided to take a chance. As he headed out into the dark street, he gave an involuntary shudder. It was partly due to the cold air and partly apprehension. *Regina is a survivor, right?*

CHAPTER 12

Sadly, no one would take much notice that Bill Walker was being held hostage at Alessandro's Cucina. With three ex-wives and four adult children who were not high on his list of priorities; it was little wonder that his family rarely gave him the time of day. These days they merely mirrored back his lack of effort at keeping in touch given their past experience of trying to maintain a relationship with him.

Bill's most recent divorce had only been settled six months ago. The bitch had ended up being no different than his first two wives. A whiny and needy pain in the ass who accused him of publicly belittling and humiliating her, lying to her and bedding other women. So what if he did those things? Didn't every man? His father certainly had and his mother stuck around until she died of a stroke recently. It would seem there was no such thing as a loyal woman anymore.

Bill was a textbook narcissist and perfectly aware of this fact. Having a conscience and doing the right thing was not high on his list of priorities. Given that Bill had done extremely well for himself in business and was rather wealthy, this was proof enough to him that karma did not truly exist. He loved the power that came with money and how all his little minions sucked up to him to try and get a piece of the action. Bill had treated his ex-wives badly and his marriages all ended on a sour note, with his bratty kids always siding with their respective mothers. They could all rot in hell as far as he was concerned. Bill was convinced he was charming and handsome despite the fact that his face showed years of debauchery including too many late nights, rich food and fine wines. He likened his wizened face to the celebrity chef Gordon Ramsay. Actually, personality-wise, he proudly considered he was probably scathing and ruthless like him too.

Bill had recently bedded a young intern named Angela who desperately hoped he would buy her a Chanel handbag. She had cooed in his ear post-sex about what a big boy he was and told him how handsome he looked with his sandy hair and distinguished looks. Using her high-pitched girly voice reserved especially for the bedroom, she'd whispered to Bill that he looked *so* noble and worldly wise while batting her full volume black eyelashes at him. What she was really thinking was that he looked just like a toad every time his jowls swung when he spoke. Angela secretly thought that the lines on his face were deep enough to fill with Polyfilla and he was about as attractive as a bulldog chewing a wasp. The truth was that Angela was a typical gold digger who liked to massage the ego of old goats who were sad enough to believe her bullshit due to their inflated egos.

Bill was well and truly sucked in by Angela's fake adoration and bought her a Yves Saint Laurent sac de jour tote bag as a gift to impress her. It was not quite the Chanel boy bag she was after, but she wasn't going to turn it down. Bill deserved the Angelas of the world – they were as bad as each other. But whenever Bill pursued young women who had integrity and showed no interest in him despite his wealth, he became self-righteous and angry when they rejected his advances. Bill would stop at nothing to get his own way and it made him a callous and dangerous man. Levi was his current obsession and given that he knew she wasn't keen; it made the lead up to claiming his prize all the more enjoyable. He wondered what her price was. *A Mercedes company car could be arranged if that would do the trick.*

CHAPTER 13

Friday 17 May 2019, 6.25pm

The chosen ones were assembled on the floor cross-legged in front of Farzad as though he was their kindergarten teacher. Each of them was desperately thinking of a way to either outsmart Farzad or win him over. Farzad's eyes were filled with undisguised hate, but his motive for the siege was still not clear to his captives. Levi was convinced that help was on the way and believed the police were in the process of discussing how to execute their grand plan. All the same, she started taking deep breaths in through her nose and out through her mouth as discreetly as possible. It wouldn't help to start hyperventilating at this point. She was doing everything in her power to remain calm. Her body felt leaden and rigid, though, and she was concerned that even if an opportunity arose where she could make a run for it, her legs may not cooperate under the circumstances.

Meanwhile, Paul was trying to take in every single detail he could about the scene. He knew how important it would be to provide information if he got out alive. He shuddered; he needed to think positively. What was it Mandy always used to say? *Your thoughts create your reality. As man thinketh, so he will become. I'm a survivor and I will live to tell the tale.* Paul knew where the power box was. If only he could get to it, he could cut the electricity off and take this bastard down when he was caught unaware. Tentatively,

Paul raised his hand, a meek expression on his face. 'I need to use the men's room,' he said in a quiet voice.

Farzad was still pacing in an agitated manner. 'So piss your fuckin' pants, cause you ain't going nowhere!' he snapped, his eyes blazing with hatred. Deflated, Paul's shoulders slumped downwards as he desperately tried to think of a plan B.

Bill looked over at Paul with contempt. *Doesn't the idiot realise that trying to go to the toilet is the oldest trick in the book? The guy obviously hasn't watched enough movies in his time! No way would a captor let his hostages loose – not even to take a lousy piss!*

Jacob pitied Paul as he noted the look of defeat cross his face when the gunman shut down his request to use the toilet. In contrast to Bill's thoughts, Jacob could see why Paul had tried this tactic. Apparently the gunman involved in the Lindt Café siege in Sydney *had* allowed hostages to use the bathroom. *There has to be something we can do to get out of this. I've never prayed before but please God, give me the inspiration in my time of need. I know I'm up myself but I'm a good guy deep down. Please get us out of this alive.*

Just when Regina was about to say something rather unwise to Farzad, a voice could be heard on a loudspeaker directly outside the entrance to the restaurant. A police negotiator spoke in a calm assertive tone. 'Put down the weapon and no one needs to get hurt. Tell us what you want and we can talk this through.' Farzad's bloodshot eyes gleamed. He was feeling super wired. The wound on his shoulder was still bleeding, though, and it was cause for concern. *Surely the old man hasn't cut me deep? He wouldn't have the balls!*

He was finally going to be famous! Knowing that he could be seen through the large glass windows, Farzad played to the TV cameras outside. The negotiator asked Farzad via speakerphone whether there was a phone they could communicate on. Farzad jerked his head wildly at the breadbasket, then nodded at Jagriti. 'You! Get your phone and tell the police what I want!'

The police established a line of communication to Farzad through Jagriti, who had no choice but to take on the role as his spokesperson. Her phone was now on loudspeaker. 'How many people are in the restaurant?' asked the negotiator.

Farzad nodded his approval for her to reply. 'Seven, including the gunman,' replied Jagriti in a calm voice that hid her inner turmoil. A cold knot of fear formed in the pit of her stomach as she spoke.

Farzad began laughing hysterically. 'She called me the gunman! I love that! Tell the police we are the Chosen Seven!' He shook with mirth. No one joined in.

CHAPTER 14

Mandy had known for weeks that something was bound to happen between her and Tony, which was why she blushed when Paul asked if there was anyone else. She was sure that Tony obsessed about her just as much as she did about him. In her mind she believed her thoughts would create her reality and the law of attraction was making it happen. For a mature woman, she was a little naïve, to say the least. When Tony discreetly asked her to join him at a nearby hotel on Friday night, she'd jumped at the chance.

Mandy was to meet Tony in the hotel lobby for drinks. When she sprayed her wrists and neck with her favourite lime, basil and mandarin Jo Malone perfume, she envisaged him wining and dining her before the chemistry all got too much and they wound up in his hotel room. Suddenly Mandy doubted herself. Was her outfit boring? Not sexy enough? Was she dressing for her age? All the insecure feelings from her single days as a young woman came flooding back to haunt her. Her mouth was dry as it dawned on her that she had been with the same man for twenty-five years. Would she know how to act with a new man? Would it be weird or would she know exactly what to do? Weren't women supposed to be super confident by the time they reached their late forties?

As she slipped her feet into her sexy patent sky-high black heels, she reminded herself that a hot young man wanted to have a romantic dinner with *her*. He'd approached her, not the other way around. Reminding herself she was a sexy cougar; she flicked her hair over her shoulder in what she hoped was a confident manner and set off to meet Tony.

Mandy was somewhat taken aback when Tony met her at the hotel entrance, his eyes darting furtively around the lobby like he was engaging in some sort of covert mission. He seemed a little curt and gruff as he led her straight to the lift. It was almost as though he did not want to be seen with her. Although the warning signs were there that she was about to be used, Mandy's ego would not allow her to compute this. *He must want me so badly if we are going straight to his room. Maybe there will be champagne on ice waiting for me and we will order food from room service after building up our appetites.*

But there were no surprises in the hotel room, no rose petals, wine or chocolates. *Paul would have made sure it was romantic if he'd arranged it.*

The set-up seemed rather impersonal and sordid given that the room was not adorned with their belongings. Mandy thought the room looked clinical with its cool, crisp white sheets, and she began to feel like a prostitute who was only there for business. Tony wanted to get straight down to it and there was little foreplay or tenderness. He did not seem anywhere near as charming or flirty as he did when he was behind the coffee machine; instead his eyes seemed hard and cold. The sex was soulless, meaningless and mechanical. Mandy did not have an orgasm. After the act, Tony rolled away from her and feigned sleep. With her mouth forming a grim line, Mandy dressed silently, realising finally that she was no more than another notch on his bedpost. She had no desire to engage with him or to set eyes on him ever again, for that matter. Talking to him would be pointless and she knew he wouldn't want to, so she'd reserve what little dignity she had left and leave him lying there as though *he* was the booty call. Feeling humiliated, used and somewhat dirty, she had a strong desire for a double shot of Glenlivet whisky and took the lift down to the bar to find a quiet corner to lick her wounds. As she travelled down in the lift, she thought how ridiculous her current situation was. Here she was, a middle-aged woman, old enough to know better, and she'd just been used in the way you would when you are seventeen and still clueless. *How absurd am I?*

To make matters worse, she was not enjoying living with her mother, who had quickly resumed her parental role as though Mandy was still her responsibility. She was currently crammed into her old childhood bedroom which was stuffed with 'bits and bobs' that her mother was hoarding. Apparently the room was to be cleared out but there was no sign of it happening soon. When Mandy had woken up that morning, she'd tripped over an ancient cuckoo clock and then stubbed her toe on her old school trombone, which was lying perilously close to the side of the cramped single bed she was expected to sleep in. *For fuck's sake! Why the hell has mum kept all of this shit? What the hell am I doing here? I can't sustain living like this.* Mandy had taken a deep breath and kept her thoughts to herself and gone to make a cup of tea. The minute she entered the kitchen, her mother had proceeded to hand her a packed lunch and help her on with her suit jacket, which was sweet, but so annoying. 'Mum, I'm not twelve, I can manage to sort my own lunch.' Mandy smiled through gritted teeth.

Her mum put on her best wounded look. 'Amanda Jane, don't get all ungrateful on me! I got out of bed especially to make your favourite cheese and pickle sandwich!' To her horror, Mandy felt herself respond like a child rather than an adult (it was freaky how easily these roles could be resumed). When she slunk out the door, she knew she was wearing a sulky expression and muttered, 'Sorry, Mum.' Mandy hugged her mother in much the same way that she used to before setting off for school each day as a child. Her mother smiled smugly and straightened Mandy's shirt collar.

Mandy fought off the urge to slap her mother's hand away and instead smiled sweetly as she got into her car. This situation was untenable. Although she loved her dear mother, this could *not* continue. Unfortunately, she and Paul were committed to paying for student accommodation and board for the boys until they completed their university degrees. This meant that they could not sell the family home and split their assets anytime soon.

As Mandy heard the ding indicating she'd reached the lobby, her thoughts returned to the present. She exited the lift and made a beeline for the bar. It was fairly empty and she found a quiet area next to a TV that no one was watching. A serious-looking news commentator was talking about a siege situation nearby at a restaurant in the city. Mandy suddenly sat up and took notice. *What the hell? This kind of stuff doesn't happen around here – not in sleepy old Adelaide!*

As the story unfolded, it transpired that police were still trying to identify the hostages, who were trapped inside by a man brandishing a firearm. Some concerned family members had come forward and advised that there was a possibility their loved ones were the hostages. It was thought at this stage that there may be others inside who remained unaccounted for. The camera did a sweep of the area outside, showing the armed police and media crews. All of a sudden Mandy sat up ramrod straight. There, in the background near the police vehicles was Paul's work van, with Townsend Electrical Service down the side. Mandy knew instantly that Paul was inside being held against his will. She drained her drink in one go and speed-dialled Paul's mobile phone several times. After receiving no reply, she jumped in a taxi to rush to the scene. *I'm being punished for ditching my husband for a fling with a jumped-up little prick who doesn't give a toss about me. What the hell have I done?*

CHAPTER 15

Jackie was starting to wonder if Jacob was coming back home as he did not appear with his takeaway as expected. She considered that maybe he'd decided to go to his mate's house instead and was not overly concerned about his absence at that point. Jackie and Colin were still avoiding each other because they were getting on each other's nerves. It was never anything serious though; most of their arguments were childish and petty, and they would end up laughing about it later. Jackie sighed and decided to tackle the mountain of ironing in the laundry in a bid to ignore Colin, who remained lying on the lounge flicking through the various Netflix titles.

Jackie glided the iron over one of Jacob's designer t-shirts, and sniggered out loud as her thoughts took her back to earlier that afternoon. Jackie and Leonie had been shopping at Kmart, and when they were at the checkout, Jackie was mesmerised by the piercing blue eyes of the twenty-year-old boy serving her. Staring at him in a trance-like fashion, she was blissfully unaware of the irritated queue of young people behind her, who in typical millennial fashion, were all in a major hurry.

The blue-eyed boy dazzled Jackie with his toothy smile. For a moment she was transported back in time and she imagined they were the same age. 'Your number?' the boy smiled at Jackie. *Oh my God! I'm old enough to be his mum and he wants my number! I've still got it!* Jackie's triumphant smile quickly disappeared when Leonie nudged her viciously in the ribs, her face bright pink with embarrassment.

'MUM!' she'd hissed. 'He means your PIN number, not your phone number!' Jackie glanced down at the EFTPOS machine in front of her. Sure enough, it was awaiting her personal identification number. Mr Blue Eyes was looking at her, a mixture of amusement and pity in his eyes. Feeling slightly mortified on the inside but at an age where she couldn't give a shit on the outside, Jackie gave a little chuckle and lowered her gaze while she punched in her pin number.

'Ah, just messing with you,' she'd said in what she hoped was a light and playful tone, while she hurriedly scooped up her items and stuffed them into her reusable environmental bag. The boy had tried to pack the items for her but she'd shoved his hand away rudely and snatched the receipt from him so that she and Leonie could quickly slink out of the store. Leonie trudged behind her mother with her head down. The muffled giggles coming from the schoolgirls next in line had not gone unnoticed.

As they walked back to the car, Leonie had confronted Jackie. 'Mum! Why are you so embarrassing all the time? You need to accept that you are ancient and stop trying to be all cool! It's actually disgusting that you would dare think someone that young would chat you up!' Jackie had merely shrugged and reprimanded her daughter for being so disrespectful. She then proceeded to mortify Leonie further by blasting the song 'Poker Face' by Lady Gaga at full volume while driving erratically all the way home. Jackie was not at all surprised when Leonie asked to stay at her friend's house after being subjected to the Kmart scenario, the joyride home and then her parents bickering over petty nonsense. It was too much in one day for the poor girl.

Suddenly Colin yelled out from the lounge room, 'Jackie – quick, come here!' Jackie smiled to herself. She knew he would come crawling eventually. He was probably hungry and hoping she would pop out for fish and chips. She sauntered through to the lounge, expecting to see Colin in his usual position sprawled out over the entire sofa with his legs crossed and his hands casually resting behind his head, but he was sitting up, leaning forward with his elbows resting on his knees, staring avidly at the TV screen instead. His expression was intense.

'What's going on?' asked Jackie.

'Shhhht,' Colin responded, flapping his left hand at her to be quiet while he used his right hand to turn the sound up on the TV with the remote control.

Colin turned the channel nine news up full blast to allow Jackie to hear the breaking story about the hostage situation at Alessandro's Cucina. 'It's where Jacob goes to pick up that fancy pasta, so he could be trapped inside!' he blurted at her, a panicked expression on his face.

'Holy cow!' yelped Jackie as she placed a hand over her mouth in shock. 'The universe is punishing me for not making dinner for my family tonight. Quick, get on to the cops now! We have to know what the hell is going on and if our boy is trapped in there!'

With a solemn expression, Colin rang the hotline provided by the newsreader and gave a description of his son. He was informed that at this stage the police were still trying to ascertain the identities of the hostages and were narrowing down all the descriptions being received from frantic loved ones who were all convinced someone dear to them was inside. So far police were able to confirm that, including the gunman, there were seven people left in the restaurant. One of the six hostages fit Jacob's description, but they could not say for certain that it was him. The serious-sounding officer explained to Colin that several camera crews were trying to get the best close-up angles into the restaurant from outside in a bid to match the descriptions from frantic callers to the poor people inside. Colin was able to describe what Jacob was wearing but the officer on the other end of the phone would still not confirm 100 percent whether this matched the description of one of the captives. The officer had learned his lesson from making a rookie error like this in the past and he was not about to repeat the same mistake.

There could be several young men of a similar height and build to Jacob wearing similar gym gear. It wouldn't do to make someone hysterical about their loved one until they could be sure it was definitely them. The police remained firm on their stance that it was 'probable' one of the hostages was Jacob, but until Jackie and Colin were interviewed by specially trained officers at the designated area, a positive identification could not be made. They would be provided with the opportunity to view the restaurant at close range so they could confirm if it was Jacob who was being held captive. After thirty frantic calls and texts to Jacob remained unanswered, Jackie and Colin began to fear the worst. They grabbed their jackets, bolted out the front door and headed for the mayhem of the city.

CHAPTER 16

Friday 17 May 2019, 6.45pm

The TV news crews were recording the same footage over and over as nothing much else was happening. Reporters clamoured like vultures in an attempt to get the best photos on their mobile phones. While there was a clear view into the restaurant through the huge glass windows, Farzad and his hostages could be seen, but only from the side, which made the identification process more difficult. The hostages' expressions of anguish were clear, however. Everyone in the restaurant was aware at this point that what was unfolding would now be projected around the world and no doubt create a global outcry. Nearby businesses and residents had been evacuated. Tactical police snipers were avidly searching for vantage points as a way to get to the gunman. The negotiator continued his quest to communicate with Farzad in a non-threatening way but was no closer to establishing what the purpose and intent of the siege was.

Feeling weary but knowing from experience that he may be trying to talk this lunatic around for hours, the negotiator tried a different tactic. 'Okay, so we still don't know your name or what you want, yet you know the whole world is watching. I'm presuming that's what you want to happen. But people will lose interest if they don't know what it is that you are trying to gain from this. If you don't tell us, then we remain stagnant like this with none of us achieving our desired outcomes.'

Farzad looked pensive while he considered the negotiator's words. His mind was becoming increasingly fuzzy from the blood loss, and the mobile phones in the breadbasket were starting to ring and bleep incessantly. It was making him crazy. He should have asked everyone to turn them off first. One thing at a time, though. He had to concentrate on his message to the world, and then he would deal with the phones.

Farzad spoke loudly and clearly into Jagriti's phone to the specially assigned police officer. 'This is an Islamic State attack on Australia because of your country's involvement against ISIS!' He paused for effect, then his voice rose several octaves as he bellowed, 'There is no God but Allah!'

The negotiator exchanged a wary glance with the other police officers in the vicinity. Noting that the gunman was advising this was a terrorist attack, the relevant authorities quietly but efficiently began to set a number of tasks in motion behind the scenes as they prepared to respond with the appropriate action.

'What is it that you want to achieve from this situation?' the officer enquired tentatively.

Becoming increasingly heightened, Farzad barked, 'I want a public apology from the prime minister for Australia becoming involved in the war against ISIS! I want him here at this restaurant to say sorry to my face or shit gets real! Put it out in the media that people need to stop calling and texting the hostages phones or they will be punished!' Farzad begun waving his weapon around wildly, causing the six hostages to duck as he swung the gun over their heads.

Farzad's face was clammy, his eyes still bulging and starting to look glassy. *Focus, focus, focus.* He looked at the time on Jagriti's phone. 'It's now 6.45pm. For every hour that passes that you haven't brought the prime minister to me, a hostage gets shot! SO FUCKING MOVE IT, YOU DOGS!' There was a deathly silence, both inside and outside the restaurant as Farzad's words resonated in everyone's minds. The hostages knew that the likelihood of his wish being met by the powers that be were extremely unlikely, no matter how many lives were at stake. The prime minister was not located in South Australia for a start, so unless he would accept a video call, contact was highly unlikely within the requested time frame. While the officers involved in the police counter terrorism operation began conferring with the Australian Security Intelligence Organisation (ASIO), and the International Criminal Police Organization (INTERPOL), frantic work was occurring behind the scenes in a bid to formally identify Farzad. It was imperative that his house be raided for more clues about his capabilities and intentions sooner rather than later. Meanwhile, tensions in the restaurant were running high as the hostages' realisation that they may not get out alive began to seriously sink in. A frantic statement was issued by police to be spread far and wide via various media platforms to let concerned parties know they must cease trying to contact the hostages via their mobile phones or the consequences could be deadly.

CHAPTER 17

Paula sat at her local hairdresser flicking through a magazine when she was tapped on the shoulder by a stern-looking woman standing behind her. Paula glanced up and quickly tried to place the woman, who obviously recognised her on sight, but it took a few seconds before it clicked who she was. Paula sighed inwardly and realised the woman was a colleague of her ex-husband, Bill. That part of her life was over and she seriously did not need any reminders. She would be polite, however. 'Hi there,' Paula smiled and glanced up at the lady, whose name had suddenly just come back to her. 'Helen, isn't it? How are you?'

Helen nodded curtly before replying, 'I'm surprised to see you here considering what's going on opposite the office. I'm in here to cancel my late-night appointment. How could I possibly be callous enough to get my hair done when my colleagues are being held hostage across the road from work?'

Paula looked up at Helen uncertainly. 'I have no idea what you are talking about Helen, I…' her voice trailed off as she saw the story being covered on the salon TV. 'Wait!' Paula pointed at the screen, which had 'HOSTAGES BEING HELD BY GUNMAN AT ALESSANDRO'S CUCINA' displayed in red capital letters at the bottom of the screen. 'Are you suggesting Bill is one of the hostages at this siege?' Paula's eyes scanned the screen rapidly as she tried to quickly ascertain what was going on. She knew the restaurant well, having dined there with Bill and several of his business associates when they were still married.

Helen looked down her nose with disdain before replying. 'Bill was having dinner with another colleague when a gunman took him hostage! As if you don't know what's going on!' Helen could not believe Paula had the audacity to get her hair done when her ex-husband was being held against his will. The contempt in Helen's voice made it clear she thought Paula was a disgusting human being. Paula stood up to face Helen and looked her square in the eyes.

'Firstly, as you can clearly see for yourself, I have only found out just this second about this situation, and secondly, Bill is no longer my responsibility or next of kin. In case you forgot, we recently went through a rather nasty divorce.' Paula was inwardly impressed at her assertive tone and was surprised that her voice wasn't shaky. The sessions with her therapist to rebuild her confidence post life with Bill were obviously helping.

Helen looked slightly taken aback but quickly composed herself. 'Oh, I forgot you were wife number three, weren't you, dear? Perhaps one of his other ex-wives will show a little more compassion than you,' She nodded curtly at Paula and after announcing loudly to the receptionist that she had an emergency situation and couldn't possibly be seen to be getting her hair done when others needed her, she promptly cancelled her appointment and marched out of the salon. The other clients jumped slightly in their seats as the bell jangled noisily when Helen slammed the door dramatically for effect. Everyone in the salon now had their eyes glued to the TV.

· · • ● • · ·

Paula sat back down in her seat in the plush waiting area but almost immediately stood straight back up, hovering hesitantly on the spot. She was waiting to feel something for Bill, to care about his welfare, but the feeling simply didn't come. She had waited weeks to be fitted in with Wilfred, the flamboyant senior hair stylist with the bizarre taste in clothes. Was she a bad person for feeling nothing for Bill despite knowing he was in danger and likely to be feeling desperate and afraid? Knowing it was unlikely that anyone else would check on his welfare, should she be responsible for doing it?

Her conscience was playing a tug of war. Suddenly, Wilfred appeared at her side, his tall lanky body encased in a regal-looking maroon and gold robe with a black mini-kilt and gladiator sandals on his bottom half. His hair was blonde, short and spikey on one side and longer on the other side with a pink fringe covering his left eye. He was renowned for his bossy streak but somehow he got away with it because no one cared to challenge him and he knew it. 'Hi dah-ling,' he singsonged in Paula's ear while he air kissed her. As if sensing she was contemplating leaving, he promptly whirled her around, shoved her in the small of her back and steered her towards a salon chair, which he all but shoved her into. He stood behind her and ruffled her hair while she faced the mirror. 'Dah-ling!' he screeched with a dismayed expression. 'What *have* you been doing? Your hair is as dry as straw and as thin as a rat's tail!' Wilfred paused and swooned dramatically for effect. He knew he was being bitchy but couldn't seem to help himself. 'We must fix this at once!' he announced boldly. 'You need post-divorce hair – yes?'

Paula smiled and knew at once she'd made the right decision to stay. She nodded obediently at Wilfred in the mirror. 'Yes, Wilfred, you are absolutely right!' Wilfred clapped his hands with glee, his gold bracelets jingling on his slender wrist. He loved submissive clients because it usually meant he could stretch his creative abilities and give them the hairstyles that *he* wanted as opposed to going along with their own dull ideas.

Wilfred was going to have fun with this one. While he set to work preparing his hairdressing tools in a haughty manner, he began to sing, 'I'm gonna wash that man right out of my hair!' Paula giggled at the fitting words and Wilfred narrowed his eyes critically as he ran his hands through her hair once more to decide on a suitable length and colour. *Jeez, why has Paula allowed herself to turn into a mousey old hag? She will look a million dollars when I'm finished with her! Hmm, she probably pocketed a million dollars after divorcing her rich prick husband. The biatch better leave a decent tip.*

CHAPTER 18

1974–1997, Iran

Farzad was raised in Iran by an abusive father and submissive mother. He was regularly subjected to physical and emotional abuse. Sometimes, Farzad's father would hang him from a large hook fixed to the ceiling by the collar of his shirt and he would remain there for long periods until the material finally gave way and he fell to the ground, hurt, humiliated, cold and hungry. If his father was feeling particularly cruel, he would force Farzad to eat poisonous plants and laugh at him when he projectile vomited them soon afterwards. Sometimes his guts would lurch so violently that he thought his stomach would be ripped out of his body along with its contents. As a result, Farzad ended up with a severe phobia of vomiting. By the time Farzad reached adolescence, he suffered with intense anger issues and no healthy outlets to help him manage this.

Farzad's brother, Basir, was executed when he was twelve years old for taking part in a robbery. As Basir had been the only other human being who understood Farzad's miserable existence, his loss had been unbearable. Farzad had a sister named Arash but she died when she was three years old due to a serious viral infection. Farzad's mother had completely shut down following her daughter's death and remained devoid of any emotion ever since. Farzad's grief for his siblings was never recognised and he grew up feeling unworthy, unloved and unsafe. He could not understand why his mother did not make him feel precious when he was the only child left. The truth was that his mother was so afraid of further loss that she remained in a zombie-like state for the rest of her days. Farzad's basic needs were never met and he only survived due to his own will to do so.

Farzad tried to engage in local ball games with the other street kids, but every time someone got in his way or prevented him from winning, he would lash out wildly. After several of his opponents ended up with broken bones and other serious injuries, he was banned from joining in. He did not have any friends and enjoyed few happy moments during his childhood. Farzad witnessed a number of children in his neighbourhood being taken to the gallows to be hanged for their crimes. The rest of the world thought that because Iranians knew no different that this was acceptable. But it was not accepted by Farzad, who harboured a secret burning rage that children were executed this way.

Farzad also had to endure listening to his father beating his mother when he was trying to sleep at night. He was sure his father was doing other unpleasant things to his mother too and subconsciously he learned that women were the lesser of the two species. When he was younger, he pitied his mother and tried to think of ways to save her, but as he grew older, he began to despise her for being so weak and permissive. If she ended up being beaten to death, it would be her own fault, as far as he was concerned.

Farzad recalled when a man in the neighbourhood had decapitated his wife and paraded her head around for anyone who wanted to see. Apparently his wife dared to refuse him his marital rights and he was making an example of what happened to disobedient wives. Their only son hung himself soon after.

By the time Farzad reached adulthood, he had no concept of any positive human traits, such as love, kindness, compassion and empathy. But he did know how to talk the talk; it was a trait that allowed him to survive. He became obsessed with the idea of leaving Iran and went to great lengths to make it happen.

In 1997, Farzad managed to seek political asylum in Australia and reinvent himself, making up fictitious stories to everyone he met. Given his growing interest in terrorism, he should have been on the radar of the Australian authorities, but it was so much easier to stay under the radar when the internet had not quite taken off yet. Somehow in the early days, he'd slipped through the net. Life was so much simpler before online searches became the norm.

Farzad accepted menial jobs when he arrived in Australia. His first job was collecting trolleys and bringing them back to the front of the local supermarket. It was a great way to watch people and fantasise about different ways he could make their lives change for the worse in an instant. If the snobby women who gave him patronising smiles while he pushed a load of trolleys past them knew what he was really thinking, they'd be shaking in their fancy boots. Most of Farzad's neighbours thought he was creepy and avoided conversing with him. This suited him just fine. He'd come this far without anyone by his side and he'd long accepted that he was destined to be alone.

CHAPTER 19

Sergeant Leonard Smythe scratched his chin thoughtfully. He was pains-takingly trying to put the pieces of the puzzle together to get a fuller picture of the gunman and his history. From the intelligence gathered so far, he did not really like the implications of what was in front of him. He stood in front of the massive wall chart that was a matrix of clues, photos and the timeline so far of tonight's events. Time was of the essence and his main concern was in relation to the lack of experience most of his officers had in siege situations. The majority of the training they'd undergone in the police academy was a distant memory, much like the legislation you had to know verbatim for the exams – one simply couldn't retain it all. The public were such armchair experts when it came to commenting on what police should or shouldn't do in these types of scenarios. Smythe knew the South Australian police force would be criticised no matter how they handled the siege, but all the same, for the sake of his conscience and for the lives at stake, he wanted to get it right.

Understanding the motives and getting into the gunman's head were paramount, but even if this was achieved, how could his officers be expected to reason with someone who was unlikely to be sane or rational? He could have all the psychobabble in the world but sometimes he thought it was pointless. He doubted it was possible to penetrate the mind of a madman and get him to do the right thing or change his mind about his quest for whatever his cause was. If it was possible, he was yet to witness it, so for now he would remain a sceptic. Smythe did respect the female police psychologist who was on board with this case, though, and he looked forward to hearing her perspective on things. He glanced at his watch as he thought of her; they were due to catch up to discuss her findings shortly.

Also up for discussion was the uncanny resemblance the gunman had to the description given by a thirty-year-old woman named Caitlin Price who had given a statement only three weeks ago about a man who had accosted her. Caitlin had been at a singles bar sitting alone in a corner when a tall, heavyset man with bulging eyes had joined her and would not leave her alone despite her politely declining his offer to buy her a drink. He was encroaching on her space, leaning over her, gripping her arm and saying crude things into her ear. Feeling panicked, Caitlin had looked around for help. The venue was particularly busy and the bar staff were run off their feet. Her friend Bree was dancing with wild abandon with some guy she had just hit it off with and was completely oblivious to Caitlin's silent pleas for her to return to the table. Caitlin felt trapped. Her instincts told her that rejection was likely to bring out the worst in this man, so she decided to try and play along with him but be ready to make a move to get rid of him. *Maybe I should get him to buy me a drink, then I can bolt out the door while he is at the bar.*

Caitlin had given an uneasy smile and looked into those crazy eyes of his. 'Actually, maybe I will have that drink. Some champagne would be nice, please.' The man had loosened his grip on her arm.

'Stay here,' he'd commanded. Caitlin had smiled sweetly. She could tell the man was heavily intoxicated as he swayed unsteadily to the bar. The minute he engaged with the barman, she made a beeline for the exit and sent Bree a frantic text message that read:

'Sorry, had to go, weirdo wouldn't leave me alone so made a run for it. Text me when you are home safely and I will do the same xx.'

Caitlin had gulped in the night air upon exiting the bar and decided to briskly walk to the busier part of the city to hail a taxi. She was cursing the high heels that were slowing her down. The bar was in a discreet laneway so she wouldn't be able to catch a cab directly outside, which was unfortunate. In hindsight she realised she should have arranged an Uber car to collect her. Caitlin had bent down to take off her heels and when she stood back up, the strange man from the bar was there, standing right in front of her, looking ominous. Caitlin had lunged backwards, a fearful look on her face, her heart thumping painfully in her chest. 'Why did you fuck off and leave me?' the man had barked, his face taut with rage.

Caitlin had looked around helplessly, but there was no one around to help her. She knew running would have been futile and trying to take him on physically would not go in her favour either. She had no choice but to appease him and play along with him.

'I'm so sorry, that was rude of me,' she had stammered. 'I uh, I'm pretty shy and I just felt overwhelmed, I didn't mean to upset you.' Caitlin's mind had been racing; she had to think fast. This man was clearly dangerous and if she hadn't played her cards right, she knew instinctively that she would be raped or murdered or maybe both. Her intuition was screaming at her to flee and every fibre of her body was on high alert. She had to stay calm, play the game and believe she could get the upper hand.

Caitlin's brother Liam lived only two blocks away. He was a black belt in karate and she could only hope and pray that if she could lure this weirdo there, that Liam would kick his ass into next week. *Please be home Liam, my life might depend on it.*

The man held Caitlin's right arm in a vice-like grip. He was staggering and his words were slurred. 'We are going back to my place, you cockteasing bitch, and I'm going to fuck your brains out.' He let out a brittle evil laugh, and then turned to stare at her for her reaction.

Hiding her repulsion and terror as much as she could, Caitlin heard herself say in a fake voice, 'That sounds like fun! Well guess what, I bet my place is closer than yours, why don't we head there instead?' The man preferred things done his way, in his bed and in his territory where he could hide any evidence. But this offer was tempting because he was feeling disorientated and his head was spinning a little from the drug and alcohol concoction he'd consumed over several hours. He glanced up, bleary-eyed, at the glare of the city lights. He could make out neon street signs, cars and people milling about, but everything was going out of focus and he was beginning to feel like he was on a merry go round that was going too fast. He didn't want the bitch to know how out of it he was. He wasn't even sure what street he was on. *Fuck it, I will make an exception and go back to her place to have my wicked way there instead.*

He knew deep down she was playing him, but she would be sorry when they reached her place. Just because she would be home, it didn't mean she was safe. 'Who do you live with?' he slurred, as thick white spittle formed in the corners of his mouth.

'I live with my flatmate, she may have to let us in because I've forgotten my key,' said Caitlin briskly. She didn't look at him for fear of what would be written on her face. She gave him a furtive glance; she thought the idea of a third person being at home might put him off, but on the contrary – he was digging that idea. A threesome could be fun, especially if he tied them both up. The man chuckled softly to himself, his eyes gleaming in the dark. They were now only a few metres from her brother's apartment. She desperately wanted to text him but knew that would be a mistake because the creep would probably crush her phone with his giant feet. *Please be home, Liam.*

As they edged closer to their destination, a random thought came into Caitlin's head. When she and Liam were kids, they were sometimes home alone due to the long hours their parents worked. They were told never to answer the doorbell unless it was rung using the code only immediate family members knew. It was three shrill presses of the doorbell followed by a double rap on the door with your knuckles. Caitlin hadn't used the code for over twenty years; she could only pray that Liam would remember it now and somehow understand she was in trouble.

They approached Liam's front door and the man's grip on Caitlin's arm was almost cutting off her circulation. She shook uncontrollably, while trying to appear unruffled. With her free hand, she pressed the bell three times and knocked sharply twice. At the very least, Liam would have to know it was her at the door. *Please be home, please be home, please be home.*

Liam sat in the lounge, binge watching *The Bodyguard* series on Netflix, a postcoital glow on his face. He and his girlfriend had recently moved in together and were still at the stage where they had constant, urgent sex at random times of the day or night and in the most obscure places. Tonight, of all things, she'd wanted to do it while sitting on top of the washing machine whilst it was on the spin cycle. It had certainly been different. Liam took a swig of beer, then sat up with a start when he heard the old childhood ring and knock combination on his front door. He remembered instantly what the code was and wondered why Caitlin would call on him late on a Friday night; it wasn't like her. He peered out through a gap in the blinds and saw a strange looking man gripping his sister's arm. He knew instantly what the scenario was and bolted down to the front door after instructing his girlfriend to stay put.

While Liam was a black belt in karate, he felt something more instant was required than his well-practiced moves. He reached for his baseball bat and swiftly opened the door, yanked his sister hard on the arm to propel her forward into the doorway and promptly smashed the creep over the head with the baseball bat before slamming the door shut. There was a silence from the other side of the door which would hopefully indicate the guy was out cold.

They were both shaking, their breathing ragged, while the adrenaline rushed through their veins. They hugged for several minutes before composing themselves and ringing the police. Once Liam's heartbeat returned to a steady beat, he grabbed his sister by the shoulders, his gaze intense. 'Jesus, Caitlin, how the hell did you end up in this predicament? That guy was serial killer material!' Liam's initial relief suddenly turned into anger.

Caitlin was hurt by her brother's words. 'Seriously Liam, I can't believe you are having a go at me! I did not want anything to do with this guy! He pursued me and would not have taken no for an answer! I had to play along in order to survive. He latched on to me and was really forceful!' Caitlin burst into tears as the enormity of her ordeal begun to sink in.

Immediately remorseful for being insensitive, Liam's expression softened. 'Oh God, I'm sorry sis, I'm being an asshole. It just scares me to death to think that something could have happened to you tonight.' Liam paused and shivered. 'To think how this could have ended… I seriously hope the cops catch him before he rapes and kills someone. I don't know what I would have done if anything had happened to you. Thank Christ I was home tonight.'

Unfortunately, by the time the police arrived to take their statements, there was no sign of the man and there was no indication he was anywhere in the near vicinity. Liam was dumfounded that a man could take a whack to the head of such brutal force and somehow get up and walk away. It was like he was superhuman. He was sure he'd knocked the perpetrator out at the very least, given that he'd fallen to the ground immediately. Due to the distinctive description of the physical and personality characteristics of the man, Smythe had a strong hunch this was the same man. The bruises on Caitlin's arm where he had gripped her were definitely inflicted by the hands of a giant brute. The police illustrator had put together an Identikit of the suspect, which was reconstructed from Caitlin's description of her attacker's facial features. It was almost identical to the description of the gunman.

CHAPTER 20

Jagriti, Paul and Jacob kept catching each other's gaze through discreet side glances and silently they formed a bond. Each knew they would be integral to what would unfold next but at this stage it was not clear how they would go about things. Paul noted his work shirt was saturated with sweat. He'd felt hot earlier but now he felt strangely cold as his clothes stuck to his skin.

Jacob felt his insides turn to liquid under the gaze of the gunman and was desperately trying to concentrate on not shitting his pants. At least it gave him something to focus on until he summoned up the strength to take action. He marvelled at Jagriti who seemed almost serene despite the situation they faced. Obviously she would not be feeling calm inside but the fact she could appear that way was making her gain the utmost respect from Jacob. He felt in awe of her. *She isn't even visibly shaking like me, what a girl!*

Regina refused to be intimidated. *If I'm going out, then I'm going out in style. Ain't no muthafucka gonna bring me down!* With her nostrils flared, she glared at Farzad defiantly and decided to speak up. 'Wait a second… isn't this a copycat of the gunman at the Lindt Café siege in Sydney? I followed that story all the way from New York City! Ain't you got your own ideas? Are you even a real terrorist? Or just a wannabe?'

There was a collective gasp of horror from the others at Regina's brazen manner and they cowered in fear, their faces screwed up, while they braced themselves for the impact of her daring questions. There was a short silence as Farzad considered how to respond.

Bill squeezed his eyes shut, lowered his head and wrapped his arms around his shins as a way of protecting himself. He was sure what the American lady had just said would impact negatively on them all and he would rather not look at what was about to happen next.

Levi was beside herself with fear, her face stricken with angst. If the larger-than-life dark-skinned lady carried on like that, they would all be doomed. She thought of her husband and daughter at home. Her family were bound to know what was happening by now. Fresh tears filled her eyes while she thought of Ben's worried face. She could envisage him chewing his cuticles nervously, an anguished expression weighing down his handsome features.

Farzad was still losing blood from his shoulder wound. It was throwing him off course and making him weak. He knew his responses were becoming slower and he could not be sure how to answer this crazy American woman. His thoughts were becoming increasingly muddled.

'Shut the fuck up, bitch, or you will be next!' he finally barked at her in a hoarse voice. Regina knew at that point that he didn't have a real answer for her and had a strong hunch he was no real terrorist. Despite Regina being tempted to antagonise him further, she refrained from responding as she calculated her next move. Farzad was irritated to note that she did not look scared and it irked him. His left eye began to twitch as he tried to intimidate her with his penetrating stare. *The bitch does not look afraid! What is wrong with her?*

Regina considered that the gunman was just some sad loser trying to get some airtime. He was a mickey mouse outfit, not the real deal. Regina's confidence suddenly grew; she could get the upper hand. She didn't know how, but she knew she would. He could have shot her just now, but he hadn't. She had tested the waters. Dudes like him liked to stick to their plans. So, if he said he wouldn't shoot someone for another hour, then he wouldn't. She put money on him being superstitious about that. In his mind, he wouldn't be taken seriously if he deviated from his plan. So that meant she had a window of time to get things under control – just under an hour, to be precise. But how best to use that time? Her mind was racing. Surviving was something she had grown rather skilled at growing up in the Bronx. Tonight sure as hell wouldn't be any different. But she needed these Australian drips on board with her. Hopefully they grew some balls real soon or someone was doomed. In fifty-three minutes, to be precise…

CHAPTER 21

Saturday 9 February 2019

Farzad had trouble attracting women and on the rare occasion he went on a date, it usually ended badly, with neither party attempting to plan any further meetings. One of Farzad's recent encounters was with a mousey-looking single mother named Natalie. She reeked of desperation, which Farzad had sniffed out from a mile away and used to his advantage. Natalie's intention was to have one or two drinks with Farzad and then return home. Her children were staying at her sister's house and she wanted to call them before they went to bed. Natalie had been badly hurt by the children's father and was cautious about dating again. She certainly had no intentions of being intimate anytime soon, because she was rather self-conscious about her body due to the deep silvery stretch marks that covered her stomach and the tops of her legs. She was lonely though, and deep down she still dreamt of finding true love, hence her occasional secret visits to the well-known singles bar she now found herself in. Natalie did not tell a soul that she frequented the singles bar and sadly this would end up being to her detriment.

Natalie's intuition didn't feel good about Farzad from the offset. There was something about his eyes – they were so cold and calculating. She made up her mind pretty quickly that she would have a couple of drinks with him to be polite and then make her excuses about getting back to her children.

Farzad had other ideas, however, and when Natalie was distracted by an incoming message on her mobile phone, he'd slipped the 'date rape drug', Rohypnol, into her glass of Moscato, then ordered a ride home via the Uber app on his phone. He knew he had to act quickly before the drug took hold. Farzad asked Natalie if she fancied moving to an outdoor table for some air and shoved her towards the exit hurriedly. The barman stopped drying the glass in his hand and watched intently, his eyes narrowed. He had a bad feeling about this guy and suspected he was up to no good. He'd been around long enough to spot a deviant, but what could he do? The police wouldn't be interested in his 'hunch' that a weird looking man coerced a woman to leave with him. Still curious, the barman walked outside, pretending to look for empty glasses for collection. He witnessed Farzad bundle the woman into the back of the waiting Uber car. He noted with unease that she looked completely out of it, despite having been perfectly coherent only minutes before. Scrabbling around in his apron pocket, he found his notepad and pen and scribbled down the registration number of the car. He felt that he had to do something.

The barman's intention was to give the details to police and if they wanted to dismiss it, at least he would have done what he could and be guilt-free. The rest of his shift was insanely busy and when he finally fell into bed at 2.00am, he made a mental note to call into the local police station in the morning. When he woke up, his girlfriend had already put a load of washing on including the apron he'd been wearing at work the night before. In her rush to get to her Pilates class, she'd bundled everything into the machine without checking his apron pocket. The registration number was no longer legible on the soggy notepad and that was the end of that. The barman couldn't decide whether to still make a report. After all, he could describe the couple, but without the registration number, there would be no way of tracking them down.

Not being one to use Ubers and a bit behind the times, the barman failed to realise that the Uber car could easily have been tracked just by providing the time, location and type of car. His girlfriend was always telling him he was still living in the olden days when it came to technology. Had he remembered to relay the story to her, she would have told him what to do. In the end, it was all too *hard and he put it to the back of his mind. He would regret this one day in the near future when the imposing looking man made headline news and his sinister image was beamed around the globe. The barman would recognise him instantly and promptly lose his appetite for his vegemite toast. The man's image would haunt him for a long time.*

By the time Farzad got Natalie into his bedroom, she was temporarily paralysed but still alert. He used his brute strength to carry her to the middle of his bed. This allowed him to do things to her that she would not have agreed to under normal circumstances. He'd stared into her horrified eyes as he crushed her with his full body weight and was fascinated by the single tear that leaked out of her left eye. He licked the tear away before rolling off her to face the other way as he gathered his thoughts. His intention was either to kill her and hide the evidence or keep her as some sort of sex slave. Because he'd exerted himself way more than he was used to, he'd made the mistake of falling into a deep sleep.

The drugs had worn off more quickly than anticipated and in the early hours of the morning, Natalie summoned all of her might to roll off the bed and escape before he awoke. Farzad was fast asleep and snored loudly, his face contorted as though breathing was an effort. Natalie's body was leaden and aching, but she knew she had to get back to her sister's house. Her children needed her and that was what she had to focus on.

First she must call the police and have this beast arrested, although she could not bear the thought of the statement she would have to give, not to mention the forensic evidence that would need to be gathered. Natalie had been a victim of a controlling man before and thought by shelving it, she could make it go away. She couldn't, and it hadn't. Vengeance for womankind was the only way forward now. Natalie stumbled out into the street, trying to figure out her location; she thought she was somewhere in the north but couldn't be sure. She was becoming short of breath and felt like her chest was being crushed by an unknown force. Shooting pains in her right arm were causing her to panic. Once safely around the corner, she called 000 and then promptly collapsed. Paramedics arrived on the scene in under three minutes to find a passer-by desperately trying to revive Natalie by applying rapid chest compressions. Sadly, Natalie had suffered a heart attack and died on the way to hospital. DNA samples were taken from her most intimate parts during the autopsy in the hope that one day whoever sexually assaulted her would one day be held accountable.

Natalie had not revealed the singles bar she was going to that night out of fear of being judged by her sister. When police turned up to visit the Chinese restaurant she claimed to have been at on the night of her death, the officers were somewhat frustrated when not a single staff member or patron could remember anyone of Natalie's description. Unfortunately, Natalie's pride had got in the way of her attacker being found and the barman who had witnessed them leaving was never interviewed because no one made the connection to the bar. Strangely, not a soul came forward from the singles bar to say they remembered Natalie being there that night.

Never being one to watch the news, the barman was oblivious to the appeal for anyone who may have known Natalie's final movements. Given that the bar he worked in was weirdo central, he managed to shelve the memory of Farzad and focus on the current stream of desperados trying to find love.

The traces of drugs in Natalie's blood and the semen samples definitely made her death appear more sinister than the initial diagnosis of a tragic heart attack. However, her death remained a mystery despite the police investigation. They were looking at the wrong CCTV recordings and therefore would continue to draw a blank. Natalie's devastated sister stepped in and took on the care of her children.

Farzad was surprisingly cool, calm and collected when he woke up to find that his victim had escaped. He neither cared for her well-being nor the likelihood that she would report him. He was arrogant and took the stance that what was meant to happen, would happen. He half expected police to burst into his house and arrest him any minute, but they never came. Rather than feeling relief, this made him angry. All he ever wanted was for the world to sit up and take notice of him. This fuelled his rage and he began to adopt extremist views. He joined a number of online groups that supported these views in order to feel included.

· · ● ● ● · ·

Farzad learned a lot from his online searches. He was furious that Iran had violated its treaty obligations. Whilst living in Australia, he'd learned of the international community that adopted human rights treaties to exclude child offenders from the death penalty. He also learned that Amnesty International opposed the death penalty and called upon the Iranian authorities to end this shameful practice. This began a love-hate relationship in his mind. He hated Iran, yet it was an intrinsic part of him. He hated Australians, yet they seemed to care about the rest of the world. All the same, the Australians were far too privileged for their own good; they were always complaining about First World problems. Farzad had to be the good that came out of all the atrocities and be the one who would wake up the rest of the world.

The need for power and control was inherent in Farzad. Since his early teens, he'd suppressed a strong desire to cause mass destruction, preferably mass murder. One day he looked up the definition of genocide and read that it meant the intentional action to destroy and kill an entire race. His pulse quickened and he felt warm and fuzzy, like what he imagined falling in love felt like. Except he was not in love with a person; he was in love with the notion of wiping out the stupid self-righteous, lazy, moronic Australians that surrounded him on a daily basis. On his own, he could not achieve much, he was well aware of that. But he would damn well be doing something, even if it was on a much smaller scale. He hated the world he lived in and begrudged people who were happy. If Farzad saw people laughing and having fun, it infuriated him beyond measure. Didn't they know how messed up Iran and Syria were? Who did Western people think they were that they should feel so joyous?

He could not ever remember feeling like life was fun, and to him, the fake people in Australia were beneath him. They had not been subjected to war, terror, children wandering the streets with missing body parts, becoming orphaned overnight, houses being destroyed and living day by day, barely surviving. They were self-righteous, entitled and would not know real horror if it came up and bit them on the ass.

Farzad despised the Australian way of life even though he knew it was a privilege to be accepted there. He followed some Australians on social media just so he could study their mindset. The Westerners wouldn't know a real problem if it smacked them in the face. He particularly despised millennials, who posted statements on Facebook such as 'FML (fuck my life) my hair straightener is broken and now my night is ruined.' People like that deserved to die – they were simply a waste of space.

Seriously, he would not think twice about snuffing out the life of these pathetic, spoiled morons. What value did these brats add to the world? Zero! They were all simpletons whose biggest problem in the world was being without Wi-Fi when it dropped out. Discipline was a thing of the past and kids were ruling the roost everywhere you turned. Farzad followed some young people in their early twenties on Instagram and howled with laughter when they described themselves as 'public figures', 'influencers' and 'entrepreneurs'. These kids thought they were moulding, guiding and shaping the world but had absolutely no clue about the real world outside the confines of their privileged lives.

They were self-obsessed and fuelled by reality shows that only served to promote droves of egotistical idiots. The IQ of society was seriously plummeting, and it was a dire situation.

Well, it was time he taught them all a thing or two about the harsh realities of life. Farzad often thought about his life's purpose. Sometimes he took concoctions of different drugs to bring out his creative mind and help him find the answers he was seeking. He had become dangerously close to killing random people he despised on sight on more than one occasion. The only thing stopping him was the fact he was superstitious and wanted everything to be just right on the night. Farzad had it in his mind that 2019 was the year of change – of that he was certain. He would execute his plan (which was not yet clear) when it came to him who the chosen ones should be. He had a large black leather-bound journal and had made entries in it every day without fail for a number of years. He had been cultivating a plan of action for some time, but somehow it never became defined. He eventually decided that certain aspects of the plan could not be deviated from (such as how many people would be involved and that he would use a firearm) but the rest would be thrown to the universe for guidance when the time was right. He knew Allah would not fail him.

Although Farzad had been writing down his ideas for so long, he never went back to read over his extensive entries. In his mind, he had been carefully planning things out over time, but the reality was that the only definite action he had documented was the fact there would be the Chosen Seven (including him). The rest was unintelligible jargon. So in his warped mind, careful plans had been unfolding, yet all he had achieved was years of stating over and over again how many victims would be at his mercy on the day of enlightenment. This would turn out to be useful for the police psychologist, although it didn't take a genius to work out that Farzad was insane and lived in some kind of warped fantasy land.

CHAPTER 22

Friday 17 May 2019, 7.15pm

Behind the scenes, the Australian Federal Police began going through their files to ascertain if there were any profiles matching those of the 'terrorist'. It was confirmed that there was an extensive dossier on a person of interest named Farzad Abed due to an attempted attack on Australian serviceman in 2008. The police commissioner was advised in a formal briefing that the images captured by the journalists stationed outside Alessandro's Cucina had been matched to the photos in the dossier. They had their man, but his real intentions were still unclear. The next step was to find his current residence and raid the property.

By 7.15pm, enough background information had been gathered by the authorities to link Farzad to a rental property in a low socio-economic area located north of the city. The estate agent who managed the rental property was already on site to let them in so that no break-in would be required, hence faster access. They had just forty minutes to come up with a solution to manage this situation before Farzad potentially took another life. The tactical team were aware that little contact was being made with the gunman and he was likely to react soon to his demands not being met. The lengthening stalemate was of concern and police hoped the gunman would become fatigued and surrender soon due to his injury. Of further concern was the need to find other suitably trained tactical officers to take over if the siege dragged on for hours on end, which was often typical in these situations. There was a duty of care to ensure the officers on duty were able to take a break. Ironically, there was not a single police officer that would realistically be able to 'switch off' if they were relieved from their duties to rest. Eventually everyone involved would tire, but none of them would sleep until it was over. Only a small section of the tactical officers were trained to deal with siege situations and there was not an abundance of trained officers to step in to relieve the current officers on duty. These officers had raised the potential risks of being such a small unit many times with the Police Association. However, like most other police forces around the world, the budget for training further specialised officers was limited and unlikely to increase until an event as big as this one forced it into action. Once again, the coroner would criticise this aspect of the case in his findings.

It did not take police long to find cause for concern after raiding Farzad's home. While he had deleted his recent browser history on his laptop, police from the electronic crime section were able to restore this just as quickly as it had been wiped. The officer in charge of the task shook his head and grimaced at the screen. *When the hell will these extremist idiots understand what digital footprint means? There is no such thing as permanent deletion! Great for us cops to bust your sorry ass but too bad for you, sucker!*

Farzad had recently taken part in several extremist videos where he described himself as a terrorist and called on all Muslims to attack the current US president. At this point, INTERPOL provided further information and the pieces of Farzad's background and upbringing were brought to the table for consideration. It was starting to look a lot like Farzad was indeed attempting a copycat of the Lindt Café siege, which had occurred in Sydney in December 2014.

·•·●·•·

Briony Murdoch was a highly experienced police psychologist. She was an attractive woman in her late forties with a glorious mane of long silky blonde hair and exceptionally large breasts. Briony was completely unaware that her male colleagues jokingly referred to her as 'Tittany Spears' behind her back. It was meant to be a term of endearment due to her likeness to the blonde singer Brittney Spears. However, no one dared tell her of the in-house joke because the reference to her large bust was unlikely to be appreciated by an educated feminist like Briony.

Briony thrived on complex criminal cases and the pressure did not seem to faze her. She confidently addressed the myriad of officers of various important titles with her theory. She stood up to her full height, tilted her chin upwards and smoothed down her black suit pants with her elegant, manicured hands. 'Okay, guys, listen up.' Briony's earnest hazel eyes worked the room, ensuring that she had everyone's full attention. 'There's no time to undertake extensive psychological profiling on the gunman. As you know, I've had to work with the limited information presented to me due to the ticking of the clock. My immediate assessment is that this guy has undiagnosed mental health issues, possibly stemming from his childhood experiences in Iran. He fits the profile of a child sociopath whose basic needs were never met due to the horrific circumstances he was brought up in.' Intrigued, the other officers nodded for her to continue. Briony grimaced and continued, 'I have deduced that Farzad may also have psychopathic, narcissistic and consequent attention seeking tendencies. This guy just wants the world to sit up and take notice. There is no definitive proof linking him to any cults or terrorist groups. Our sources indicate he operates as a one-man show. While he concurs with other extremists online and attempts to join in with them, it does not look like anyone has accepted him or taken him too seriously at this stage. This will have undoubtedly hurt his ego and increased his desire to be noticed and prove his mission.'

Briony shifted her weight from her left to her right foot before continuing. Her feet were killing her but for some reason she insisted on wearing high heels when addressing a predominantly male group. They made her feel powerful, and if she was honest, she enjoyed emphasising that smart women could also be feminine. This was perhaps slightly hypo-critical, given that she portrayed herself as a raging feminist when it suited her. Her eyes swept the room and she maintained eye contact with Superin-tendent John Marshall for longer than necessary. Tilting her chin, she spoke in the self-assured voice she reserved for addressing her colleagues.

'This provides some hope to the authorities, because while he is still armed, dangerous and clearly capable of cold-blooded murder, it does not appear at this stage like he is part of a bigger plan with other contenders.' Briony chewed her bottom lip thoughtfully. 'Much like the Lindt Café siege situation, we need to seriously consider whether we use an Emergency Action Plan to storm the restaurant due to the crisis situation. Or, are we are able to continue with the earlier plan of Deliberate Action, which includes a carefully crafted rescue attempt? Let's be honest here, we are all hoping for a window of time where the gunman gets distracted and we can move in. However, time is of the essence and the reality is that we are going to be heavily criticised if we stand back and watch this unfold without taking action for too much longer. We have already had two fatalities tonight and the gunman has not allowed any access to the bodies. This has got to be freaking those hostages out something terrible. We can only imagine the terror and frame of mind of the remaining captives.'

When the room got loud with words of protest and differing theories regarding the best approach to contain the siege, Briony held up a hand authoritatively and raised her voice significantly in order to be heard. 'We already know that no matter how we handle this situation, we will be damned if we do and dammed if we don't take action. I know that my role as a psychologist is not normally required to become involved in what type of action is taken, but I've specifically been asked to comment on this unique situation. Each possible approach has its own risks, but we absolutely cannot, I repeat *cannot*, keep watching this unfold without reaching a definitive agreement on how best to act moving forward.' Briony paused, looking out the window thoughtfully. 'I do question how this man was able to enter Australia when it is clear he is of dubious character, but that is another matter entirely.'

As the group stood, silently digesting this information, a young male police officer who was on the receiving end of incoming information regarding the raid on Farzad's home suddenly burst in. 'Sir!' he addressed Marshall directly given that he was the chairperson of the meeting. 'We found an item of interest under the gunman's mattress! He keeps a journal called 'the Chosen Seven'!' The young officer became breathless as he was desperate to impart his newfound knowledge quickly to his waiting superiors. He took a deep breath before continuing. 'It mentions his intention to change the world but not until he finds the perfect six hostages to make his dream a reality. Including him, they are to be known as 'the Chosen Seven'. He dreams of this headline on newspapers around the world. This guy is as mad as a cut snake!'

Marshall nodded brusquely at the wider group. 'Okay, this is a new piece of vital information that needs to be discussed by the task force. In light of this latest news and the information provided by Tit ... uh ... Briony, let's get back to our posts and add these pieces to the puzzle. Meanwhile, a separate team is working hard to ensure we have the correct identities of the six hostages so we can eliminate the torrent of names being put forward by concerned members of the public.' Marshall clapped his hands authoritatively. 'Time is of the essence, guys, let's move it!' Within thirty seconds, the group had disbanded, each scurrying back to their relevant posts to examine the new information further.

As Marshall walked away, he had a sudden, vivid flashback to twenty years ago. He'd just graduated from the police academy and Briony had just finished her psychology degree. They'd wound up in the same bar during their respective celebrations and gone back to his place for a night of passion. The sex had been mind-blowing and he'd never experienced anything like it since. Each one too proud and egocentric to approach the other, neither of them pursued each other or mentioned that night again despite their obvious chemistry. Their careers had been intertwined for over two decades and they'd managed to stay professional and act like it never happened. Sometimes Marshall would watch Briony with lust in his eyes when she gave her expert opinion on the latest heinous perpetrator, but he gave nothing away. The truth was that he would give anything to be pounding into her and crushing those gigantic tits again. To make matters worse, Briony had become sexier with age. However, being the upstanding citizen of the community that he was, he put such thoughts to one side. Ignoring the unwelcome erection bulging in his pants, he allowed himself to indulge in the memory for a minute or two then proceeded to roll his sleeves up in anticipation of becoming one of tonight's hero's. *Hell, if I can get this siege under control and get back in the limelight, my wife might let me back in the marital bed. It's unfortunate that she has bee stings for tits but hey, I guess I can't have it all in life.*

CHAPTER 23

Friday 17 May 2019, 7.15pm

Farzad paced up and down hyperactively, continually asking Jagriti the time every few seconds. He was feeling like a fraud and his euphoria at having killed the couple earlier was fading because he had no idea what his next move should be. He knew he would not hear from the police until the hour was nearly up because they would be too busy doing everything in their power to bring the situation under control while they liaised with the office of the prime minister. He also knew that his hostages were bound to try something to stop him soon as it was obvious that he was weakening. His blood loss seemed to have slowed down, but he was still a terrible sight. His clothes were now heavily stained with bright red patches. He hoped that it was not too obvious that he was struggling to keep holding the gun upright.

To distract them, he decided to learn everyone's name and demanded each of the hostages tell him a little bit about themselves. Reluctantly, they did as they were told. Using his gun, he pointed it at them in the order he wanted them to speak. 'You!' he barked at Regina. She certainly had intrigued him earlier with her bold manner and bad ass attitude.

Regina rolled her eyes to indicate that she felt like a high school student being reprimanded by a schoolteacher. She straightened her back, assuming a bold and confident air. 'My name is Regina and I'm from New York City.

I'm here on a work visa. Let me tell you my home city has been to hell and back and I ain't got no fear left. I sure as hell ain't scared of you!' She stared defiantly around the room, expecting others to nod in agreement, but no one would dare meet her eyes.

Farzad's left eye twitched. He found it difficult to think of the best way to respond to this foul woman. Regina waited for the gunman to bite back. Strangely, he didn't, and she was secretly disappointed. Using the opportunity to move on to the next person, Farzad merely nodded in a disinterested fashion and looked pointedly at Jagriti to indicate she was to speak next.

Jagriti was able to maintain her cool, calm and collected façade while she spoke. 'I'm Jagriti, I study nursing at Flinders University and I work part-time in this restaurant.' Farzad nodded dismissively, then nodded at Paul to indicate he should speak next.

Paul visibly tensed, his jaw throbbing due to it being so tightly clenched for so long. His eyes remained hard. 'I'm Paul, I'm an electrician and came here tonight to drop off a quote, looks like I picked the wrong night to pop in,' he said wryly, a hint of sarcasm evident in his tone. Farzad nodded once more, then looked directly at Bill.

Bill looked pensive; his white face was pinched. He held the view that he could buy his way out of anything; it was something his father had taught him. Most situations could be rectified, and the majority of people could be won over when you waved a few hundred dollar notes at them. The lunatic gunman would be no different. Bill spoke up in what he hoped was a friendly 'man-to-man' voice.

'Hey, my name is Bill and I'd just like to say that whatever your cause is, I'm happy to donate some serious funds to it, like uh thousands of dollars. So uh, if it's money you need, then I'm your man. Maybe we can sort something out and we can all go home?'

Farzad stared at Bill with contempt. The stupid prick was meant to inform him about himself and had failed to do so. Instead he had been foolish enough to think he could negotiate with him. 'What I want goes much deeper than money and that's what you Westerners don't fucking understand!' Farzad snarled. Impulsively, he marched over to Bill and whacked him hard with his gun in the left side of his head, knocking him out cold.

'Oh Jesus!' whimpered Levi in horror, as she witnessed her boss topple over and slump sideways onto the floor. Silence descended over the restaurant once more.

Farzad was becoming weaker. He lowered himself slowly to a seated position on the floor, his eyes trained on the sea of faces swimming in and out of focus in front of him.

Realising she better comply with the gunman's request in order not to suffer a similar fate, Levi quickly told the group her name and explained in a shaky voice that she was there to have a business dinner with Bill, who was her boss. Farzad nodded pompously, noting with glee how fearful this Levi lady sounded. Jacob spoke next. He was nervous and couldn't seem to articulate the best way to reply. 'I'm Jacob, I'm a personal trainer, I came here tonight for the low carb zoodle pasta.'

Regina stifled the urge to giggle at such an inappropriate time, but she found Jacob's comment rather amusing. He obviously just blurted that out due to nerves, but seriously was he so up himself that he thought anyone cared what kind of pasta he ate? Even now in this crazy situation, he had to justify his dinner choice by mentioning it was low carb. She made a mental note to give him shit if they got out of here alive. Regina had a terrible habit of laughing during serious situations and if she was honest with herself, it was usually down to nerves. Not much fazed her in life and feeling nervous was rare, but she was experiencing teeny tiny ripples of anxiety due to the close proximity of the madman's gun. She was able to talk herself out of it pretty quickly, though. She closed her eyes to gather her thoughts. *NO!* she thought. *I won the badass of the Bronx title and I'm gonna straighten my damn crown right now! I won't go down without a fight!*

'Okay, here's the deal,' Farzad addressed the group authoritatively. The hostages looked on with dread. 'My name is Farzad and *you* have been carefully selected with the guidance of Allah to form the Chosen Seven. I want you to know that it was Allah's wish for each of you to be chosen; it is fate. I saw something in all of you and tonight you will all work with me and follow my orders so that together we can change the world forever!'

There was a stunned silence while the group processed this. It was clear to all of them (except Bill, who remained unconscious) that the gunman was a complete lunatic with serious mental health issues. Silence ensued for almost a minute while everyone considered what an appropriate response to this apparent honour might be. Jagriti put her hand up. Farzad nodded at her, intrigued to know what the mousey Indian girl might have to say. Jagriti knew she had to pretend to be on her captor's side to win him over. She spoke in a quiet but assured tone. 'I'm honoured you saw something in me and picked me to be one of the chosen ones. As you know, I'm a student nurse so let me use a tablecloth to dress your wound. You have been bleeding quite profusely. If I can help you gain strength and stop losing blood, you will be in a better position to guide us through our mission.'

Farzad nodded thoughtfully to indicate his approval and allowed Jagriti to grab the nearest tablecloth to make a tourniquet for his wounded shoulder. He was pleased with what she'd said and decided he trusted her. While she dressed his wound, Farzad was momentarily distracted. Seizing the opportunity, Jagriti deliberately blocked Farzad's view from the others while she tended to his injury. She glanced briefly at Paul, who nodded to indicate he understood the message she was trying to convey. There was a miniscule window of time that the lunatic would be distracted and he picked up on what Jagriti was trying to do loud and clear.

In the fifty seconds or so that Jagriti blocked her captor's view, Paul deftly sprinted to the breadbasket and grabbed his phone. Thank God it had a distinctive green phone cover and could be quickly identified. He spotted a dropped fork under a nearby table and quickly stuck it down the front of his pants. Although this had only taken a matter of seconds, Paul was sweating profusely when he sat back down in his spot. His heart was beating wildly at the thought of Farzad noticing he had moved. Somehow Paul managed to type out a frantic text to Mandy within the few seconds he had spare. Even though they were not together, she was still the mother of their boys, and he knew she would be distraught. Thankfully, Farzad did not register any movements, mainly because he was starting to lose what little wits he had left.

CHAPTER 24

Leonie and Carla were curled up on Carla's bed, surrounded by empty popcorn packets and chocolate wrappers. They were best friends, and their mums had also become close, which made regular sleepovers easy. The Ed Sheeran and Justin Bieber song 'I Don't Care' blared from a Bose sound system perched on a chest of drawers. They were giggling incessantly while they alternated between listening to music, watching Chris Lilley's TV show *Lunatics* and prank calling two hot boys from their home group at school. It was Carla's turn to choose a *Lunatics* clip. Her favourite character was Jana the pet psychic and every time she watched a clip, she would roll around laughing, clutching her sides. 'Have you seen this one?' Carla nudged Leonie. Jana the psychic was 'reading' a dog and announced to its owner, 'He's telling me your husband likes to play with himself a lot when you are not here.'

Leonie and Carla simultaneously began shrieking with laughter and jumped guiltily when Carla's mum, Sue, popped her head around the bedroom door. Carla winced because she thought her mum was going to tell her off, given that she believed the TV show was inappropriate for fourteen-year-olds. Sue looked worried rather than angry, however, and asked if she could speak with Leonie in private. Leonie glanced nervously at her friend. *What the hell? Am I in trouble with Carla's mum?* Leonie looked at Carla for support, but she looked equally baffled. Carla had no idea what her mum could possibly want to talk to her friend about. *Unless it's to discuss a secret surprise she is planning for me.*

Leonie jumped down from Carla's bed and followed Sue down the hallway to the lounge. 'Sit down, sweetie, I need to talk to you about something.' Leonie frowned, confused. *Is that sympathy I can detect in her voice?* Suddenly Leonie felt a sense of foreboding and had a hunch that whatever Sue was about to say would not be good.

Sue turned to face Leonie and took both of her hands in her own. 'There's um, uh, there's a situation in the city... at a restaurant. Your brother Jacob, he um, he is trapped inside.' Sue squeezed Leonie's hands hard without realising she was doing so. 'Your mum and dad, they are there, on standby, to make sure he is okay and they want you to stay here for as long as you need to.' Sue tried to smile reassuringly at Leonie, but her eyes were full of fear.

Leonie snatched her hands away, her eyes filling instantly with tears. 'What do you mean, Jacob is trapped? Is there a fire? Where is he exactly?' Leonie sprung up from the sofa and blurted, 'I want to be with my family, I need to know what's going on... I don't want to stay here.' Leonie scrambled frantically towards the front door, desperately speed-dialling Jackie's number.

Sue quickly followed Leonie but after realising she had connected with Jackie; she took a respectful step back to allow her friend to explain to her daughter what was happening. It would seem that Jackie was not doing a great job of reassuring her daughter because Leonie quickly became hysterical and started sobbing whilst frantically trying to unlatch the front door. When Jackie continued to insist that Leonie had to stay put, Leonie hung up on her and threw the phone on the floor in frustration. Realising she had no money and no way of getting to the city, Leonie slid down the wall, wailing loudly.

The noise prompted Carla to come out of her room. Initially she'd thought her mum was maybe trying to plan something radical for her upcoming fifteenth birthday, so she'd tried not to be nosy. But after hearing a commotion despite playing loud music, she popped her head out of her room and noted Leonie slumped on the floor in the hallway, crying. 'What the hell?' Carla was shocked to see the drastic change in her friend, who only minutes before had been so happy and full of laughter.

Fresh tears spilled from Leonie's eyes when she saw the look of concern on Carla's face as she rushed over to hug her. Suddenly Leonie felt like she was three years old and wanted the comfort of her own parents badly. Jackie made the mistake of telling her daughter that the situation was all over the news. Now Leonie desperately wanted to see it, despite Sue telling her it might make her feel worse. Leonie stood up clumsily, wiping snot and tears from her face with the back of her sleeve. She rushed back into Carla's bedroom and snatched up her laptop from the bed to Google the news. Sue tried to intervene. 'Is that a good idea, sweet…' she was interrupted abruptly by Leonie.

'I'm watching it, end of story!' she snapped somewhat fiercely. Sue understood and was not offended but Carla was a little put out that her friend was being so rude to her mum.

Carla hesitated. On the one hand, she wanted to stick up for her mum and tell Leonie not to be so cheeky because her mum was only trying to help, but on the other hand, she knew she would probably act the same way if the roles were reversed. Carla glanced at Sue and they both shrugged helplessly while secretly agreeing that there was little they could do to stop Leonie from following the news updates.

While Sue looked helplessly on at Leonie, she reflected on what a tender age fourteen was. One minute, they thought they were all grown up and knew everything. Yet in an instant, they switched back to being childlike and needy when faced with something they couldn't handle due to their lack of maturity. Sue's strong maternal instincts meant that she desperately wanted to hug Leonie but felt sure she would see this as a sign there was something serious to worry about. Instead, she played it casual, hung back and let her know she was there if she needed her.

It didn't take Leonie long to find umpteen news stories and terrorist theories online. This prompted fresh tears and feelings of panic. Finally she allowed Sue to hold her and stroke her hair while she poured out her anguished thoughts about what might happen to her big brother. It was obvious she idolised Jacob despite the regular fights they had. Sue lay in between the two girls on the bed, an arm around each of them. She could only hope and pray that the siege situation would come to a head soon and that by some miracle the remaining hostages would come out alive.

CHAPTER 25

Friday 17 May 2019, 7.20pm

An hour and twenty minutes had passed and everyone's nerves were becoming frayed. A solution to the problem was yet to manifest. The air reeked of desperation and despair. Specially designated police officers set up an area for the families of the hostages in an empty office space adjacent to the restaurant. The tension in the room was running higher with each passing minute. There was a constant crackling of police radios and officers furtively walking off with their heads down. They seemed to have mobile phones glued to their ears and adopted a hopeful look whenever a call came through from their superiors to update them. Unfortunately, the updates were still not forthcoming with a definitive plan of action. The officers placed with the hostages' relatives were filled with dread every time they clicked off their phones with nothing positive to report. It was heartbreaking looking at the sea of anxious faces with pleading eyes full of hope that willed them to have some good news.

Jagriti's parents had been first to arrive, followed by Paul's estranged wife, Mandy, Jacob's parents and finally a frantic Ben who'd had trouble finding a babysitter for Charlie. The only two hostages with no representation were Bill and Regina. Zion was now in regular contact with police and was weighing up whether or not to book a flight to Australia. He had no idea where he would get the funds for this and felt he was letting his sister down. One or two colleagues came forward to check on Bill's welfare, but it was more from a duty of care perspective than from genuinely caring about him on a personal level. Other than his most recent ex wife Paula, none of his family knew he was missing at this stage and given the way he generally treated them, they were unlikely to care.

The general vibe in the room was turning from fear and nervous energy into outrage. After the first five minutes of waiting already felt like a lifetime, Colin felt the need to speak up. He marched up to the nearest police officer and pointed at his watch. 'It's now 7.25pm and we have twenty minutes before someone in there gets shot if this lunatic keeps to his proposed timetable. It could be my son, Jacob, or it could be someone else's loved one in this room. You can't just keep us in the dark. GIVE US SOME DAMN ANSWERS!' Colin was becoming heightened and his face was bright red with exertion.

The officer he addressed was a sassy young female constable in her mid twenties named Tara Whitworth who was secretly feeling way out of her depth. 'I completely understand, sir, and I only wish I could give you the answers you seek, but at this stage all I can assure you of is the fact that everyone and their dog is doing all they can to get this under control. That includes the office of the prime minister.' Constable Whitworth used a gentle but firm tone as she placed a hand over Colin's shaking forearm.

Ben joined them. 'Well, this guy is right!' he pointed at Colin. 'My wife is in there, we have a little girl, I can't lose her, I can't think of....' Ben broke down and began to sob. Keerti, Mandy and Jackie immediately surrounded him to offer hugs and words of support. They were all mothers and their collective maternal instincts kicked in. Subconsciously, it made them feel better to nurture this man because the ache to do so for their own loved ones trapped in the restaurant was leaving a gaping hole in their hearts. They stood for several seconds in a group hug, all of them silently praying. Ben was grateful for their kindness and reminded himself to focus on the relief he'd felt when he'd discovered that the couple who had been shot were not Bill and Levi as he'd first thought. He then felt instantly guilty for being glad when the couple's death was clearly going to be devastating news for their family.

Mandy's phone dinged indicating an incoming text message. She moved away from the group to read the text. Her eyes rounded in disbelief and her hands shook when she spoke up. 'Guys! I have a message from my ex, Paul, who is trapped inside! He says to tell loved ones not to keep ringing and texting as its making the gunman mad. Apparently, he took all of their phones but Paul managed to steal his back.'

Mandy trembled as she continued. 'He reckons the gunman is weakening due to an injury and Paul is biding his time so that he can take him down when the gunman loses his concentration. Paul has a fork he can use to protect himself. He also says that he thinks the gunman is losing all sense of time and appears to have no exit strategy in place. The strain is taking its toll and Paul is worried about the effect on everyone. He is relying on the others to stay strong.' Mandy clapped her hand over her mouth in horror as she took it all in. She took a deep breath, and then continued in a shaky voice, 'Paul says he has no doubt one of them will be killed when the hour is up and wants to know what the hell police are doing?'

Tears were flowing down Mandy's face at this point while she looked accusingly at Constable Whitworth, then roared, 'WHAT THE HELL ARE YOU GUYS DOING? WHY HAVE THE POLICE NOT SHOT THE GUNMAN?' Feeling crazed, Mandy charged at Whitworth headfirst into her chest, but the young officer was too quick for her. Using a technique, she had learned at the police academy, she deftly spun Mandy around into a bear hug. Whitworth stood behind Mandy with her arms wrapped around her from the back and held Mandy this way for almost a minute before she stopped struggling and finally sagged with despair, sobs wracking her body. Once again, Jackie and Keerti joined Mandy and the three women cried, hugged and consoled each other, mirroring the anguish that each of them felt in that moment.

Whitworth knew that there were trained officers with Glock pistols and MA assault rifles at the ready. They even had three magazines ready to reload their rifles to be on the safe side, but what use were they when it seemed that no one in command seemed able to make a clear-cut decision about how to handle this guy? Although she had not been a police officer for that long, she came from a long line of police in her family and knew enough to figure out that this situation was one big mess. It was becoming increasingly obvious that no one in a position of authority felt competent or decisive enough to come up with a foolproof plan of action. As long as the general public thought that the police and other relevant government authorities were doing everything they could to save the hostages, that's all that mattered at this point. They were all just playing the game.

Whitworth felt like a fraud standing there in her uniform. It was almost as though she was playing a part in a bad TV drama. She was reminded of her brother Jimmy who shuddered every time he got on a train because he'd been a railway train mechanic and knew only too well what could go wrong with them. Blissfully unaware of the workings of a train, she'd become irritated with Jimmy every time he'd lamented that ignorance was bliss. Jimmy would try but fail not to wince at every weird clunking sound he picked up on when they'd travelled together to visit their parents. Whitworth remembered waving a dismissive hand at his concerns and saying flippantly, 'We are only going from Seaford to the city – what can go wrong?' As it happened, the train had broken down on the same line the following week and Jimmy was full of self-importance. 'I told you so!' he'd said, with a triumphant smirk on his face.

Now she knew only too well what he was talking about when it came to job-related information that you'd rather not share with the public. *What you don't know can't hurt you.... I hate knowing that these people think police are invincible and can fix everything because the truth is that we can't. I just know the way tonight ends probably won't be pretty.*

Whitworth's colleague, Constable Ross Taylor, interrupted her thoughts as he addressed the group of gathered relatives. 'Okay, guys, let's try and keep as calm as we can. I know it's easier said than done, but I do have a small snippet of news.' A hush descended on the room and all eyes became glued to his face, their expressions conveying how hungry they were for answers. Taylor continued, 'We now know exactly who this guy is and that he had this idea about forming a group of hostages, which including him, would be named the Chosen Seven. While he claims to be a terrorist, he does not appear to have any real affiliation with anyone of concern.' Taylor coughed nervously and the strain of his job was evident.

He inhaled sharply before continuing, 'Police snipers have him in their line of fire and if necessary, they will shoot. While it is obvious that the prime minister cannot realistically attend in the timeframe the gunman has demanded, he has agreed to do a video link or anything else in his power that will appease the gunman.'

All at once, everyone in the room fought for attention, firing a barrage of questions and indicating their outrage. A few insults were hurled in response to Taylor's speech. The hostages' loved ones were becoming increasingly agitated. Whitworth was inwardly shaking her head because she was pretty sure her colleague had revealed too much and misunderstood his instructions on what to tell the relatives. Now they would have to deal with the aftermath.

CHAPTER 26

Friday 17 May 2019, 7.30pm

Finally, after a painfully long ninety minutes, the police negotiator spoke with Farzad and advised that representatives from the prime minister's office were willing to talk to him via video link if he released the hostages and put his weapon down.

'NO! I WANT WHAT I ASKED FOR, YOU DUMB FUCK!' screamed Farzad into the phone. He shook with fury at the audacity of the South Australian police force, who had not obeyed his commands. When the negotiator calmly explained that it was not logistically possible to fly the prime minister to South Australia due to him being out of the country at present, Farzad shook his head violently, spraying spittle as he snarled, 'It's the prime minister or nothing!' His hostages cringed with the painful awareness that this was not going to plan and one of them was likely to be one step closer to their death. Before the negotiator could reason with him any further, a commotion ensued.

'FUCK THIS, YOU MUTHAFUCKA!' Regina suddenly screamed. She'd had enough of exercising restraint. Without fully thinking of the consequences, she leapt up and threw herself at Farzad, plunging her talon-like nails straight into his cheeks, immediately drawing blood. Stunned and caught off guard, Farzad yelped in pain, blindly firing his gun. Regina had brazenly miscalculated that he wouldn't shoot her and regret showed on her face when she fell to the floor.

'American bitch!' he hissed as he put his free hand up to touch his tender, bleeding face. There was a collective horrified gasp in the room. Regina was face down, and it was unclear where she had been shot and whether or not her injuries were fatal. The remaining captors became increasingly despondent and desperate. They knew they had to overcome Farzad as soon as possible – but how?

Farzad was furious. He had shot someone before the hour was up due to the interfering fat American woman and now his plan was in complete disarray. She was one of Trump's people; it was no surprise that she was a moron who dared to challenge him and was stupid enough to think she could get the better of him.

Farzad knew he would lose the trust of the police, because in their view, he had not stuck to his side of the bargain. Part of him felt like just blowing everyone to smithereens, including himself, right this second. It would still make him world-famous, after all. People would talk about it for years and it would make him a true martyr in the name of Allah. His hostages' relatives would be gutted. Maybe their lives would be miserable like his had been, and that in itself would make things fairer. Yes, this might be a good idea! *But wait! Allah wanted me to write the Chosen Seven plan so it would go down in history. The words in that plan are as important as the bible itself! Focus, focus, focus! The plan is the only way to proceed. I need to get back on track! All I know is there has to be seven of us mere mortals. The rest of the plan is a mystery. Let it unfold like it should at the hands of almighty God.* Farzad had no comprehension that his thoughts were insanely contradictory. He was following a plan that had no outline whatsoever.

· · ● · ·

The gunshot was heard loud and clear outside the restaurant and once again panic ensued. The only small mercy for the loved ones gathered with police was that it was quickly conveyed that the lady who'd been shot was not represented in the room the relatives were gathered in. Each of them felt guilty for their relief and secretly selfish. The truth was that they were glad the victim was an American woman whose only family member was in New York and unable to join in the collective hysteria. But it also reinforced to them that one of their loved ones was likely to be next if the situation was not brought under control in a timely manner.

CHAPTER 27

Friday 17 May 2019, 7.40pm

Jacob kept trying to make eye contact with Paul in the hope that they could use telepathy to decide what to do next. There was no doubt they were the two strongest males in the room, Paul mentally, and Jacob physically. The look that passed between Jagriti and Paul earlier was not lost on Jacob and he wanted in on the action too. After having little success in catching anyone's eye, Jacob tentatively put up his hand.

Farzad gave an abrupt nod, indicating Jacob could speak. 'Hey man, if you want to get the police back on your side, you have to let them know that was an accident when you shot the American lady. The hour is just about up and your plan hasn't gone to schedule – surely rather than shoot one of us in …' Jacob paused as he glanced at his sports watch with dread, and gulped, 'ugh surely, rather than kill one of us within the next five minutes, you can buy back their trust by not taking any more lives instead.'

Farzad considered that Jacob had a point. 'You!' he nodded at Jagriti. 'Tell them the foolish American woman attacked me and that's why I shot her. Tell them a fresh hour starts at 7.45pm.' When Jagriti did not look as impressed with his kindness as he expected her to, he screamed, 'DO IT, DO IT, DO IT!'

Frantically, Jagriti jumped to attention and called the negotiator to relay what had happened and what Farzad's were intentions moving forward. Farzad refused point blank to allow the paramedics waiting outside to tend to Regina. 'Please get him access to the prime minister somehow or we will all die,' Jagriti whispered hoarsely as she clicked off her phone.

Paul glanced at Jacob admiringly. *Nicely played, mate, it is now roughly a minute off the next scheduled shooting. The kid with the muscles has just saved our asses. Maybe there is more to him than biceps after all.*

Jagriti spoke up in a quiet but firm voice, 'I need to charge my phone because it is almost flat, can you allow me to do so behind the counter please? I know where there is a charger that staff use. I can't continue to speak to police on your behalf without it.' She spoke calmly, reassuringly in her best calm nurse's tone. It was easy to trust this unassuming girl with the medical knowledge. Farzad nodded weakly, fatigue once again getting the better of him. He knew it was unwise to let anyone out of his sight, but by the same token, how could he negotiate with police with no phone handy? His own phone had gone flat early on in the piece. This was a major oversight on his part and he was mighty pissed off about it. He had no choice but to trust the girl. She was nothing but a scared little mouse – she posed no threat and appeared to be a pious do-gooder. What harm could it do to allow her a minute's reprieve to charge her phone?

Jagriti glanced at Paul and then Jacob – both were staring at her imploringly as she deliberately took her time standing up to head towards the counter. Both men sensed she wanted to use this opportunity wisely and would need their assistance. Paul mouthed at her, 'Do you know where the power box is?' Jagriti gave a curt nod. She knew it was on the wall near the entrance, which wasn't too far from the counter. Both Jagriti and Paul simultaneously glanced at Jacob, instinctively knowing they would need his strength. Jacob winked to indicate he was on board. None of them knew for certain what the others were planning, but survival was the common denominator and they could only pray they were all on the same page somehow.

Bill started to regain consciousness after his whack to the head. He was way too groggy to focus on what was happening around him and was feeling vulnerable. It was not a feeling he was familiar with, and it scared him. Instinctively, he reached his hand out to Levi. Although Levi despised Bill, she was too decent a human being not to help him in his time of need. Levi had gone into a trance-like shock, and she knew deep down that if they did get out of this awful situation it was highly unlikely it would be on the her or Bill's merits. Levi was talented at many things but she had never felt so dumb or helpless as she did in this instant. Why was her survival mode not kicking in? Why was she not hypervigilant and filled with adrenaline and escape plans? She felt numb and frozen with shock, unable to think of a way out of this nightmare.

Levi squeezed Bill's hand to indicate her support and he gave her a weak smile to convey his gratitude. They sat like statues, side by side, each with their own private thoughts swirling around in their heads. Levi was silently praying that she got to see her baby girl grow up and reach old age with her husband. Her heart ached with the strong possibility of tonight's final outcome. She was wishing she had not followed the Lindt Café siege story in December 2014 so closely because it was feeling too close to home right now. She shuddered and shut her eyes, praying that the dark-skinned lady was still alive. They needed someone fearless like her to help them get out of here. *Please let someone in here be the hero of the night because I don't think it is going to be me or Bill.*

As Bill's consciousness slowly became sharper and his thoughts more focused, he considered that there would be friends and relatives on standby nearby. They would no doubt be out of their minds with worry. He wondered who had showed up for him. His thoughts went to wife number one, wife number two and then wife number three. *Nope, nope, nope. I'm not on good terms with any of them.* Bill then considered his adult offspring, Toby, Liam, Gerald and Monique. *Nope, nope, nope, nope.* Bill never took his father's calls these days so it was likely that he too had given up on him. A feeling of dread stole over him as he considered his poor relationship with his ex-spouses and children. His mother had passed away recently and his father rarely watched the news these days so it was unlikely he would know what was going on even if he did care. An unwelcome voice was prickling his subconscious. *It's my own fault, I treat my family like shit and never give them the time of day, why would they be there for me now?*

Outraged at his own thoughts, Bill shook his head vigorously as though to be rid of them. The whack to the head had clearly made him delirious. Of *course* some family members would be waiting with bated breath to hear of his fate. What kind of family would they be if they didn't care? There was Angela too, the intern who was madly in love with him. Hell, he had even thought about making her wife number four. Yes! Of course Angela would be there – she would run into his arms when he was finally freed and then he would be a bigger hero in her eyes than he already was. Still, the voice in his head remained. *No one will be there for a nasty piece of work like me.*

·· • ◉ • ··

Jagriti surmised that perhaps she genuinely should put her phone on charge given that it was down to 25 percent power. Then she grimaced when she realised that wouldn't work in accordance with her next move. She approached the counter and Farzad craned his neck slightly to watch her, but quickly turned back to face the others due to his reluctance to take his eyes off the wider group. Jagriti hovered near the area the charger was located at to give Farzad a false sense of security and then quickly darted over to the power box on the wall. In one swift movement, she flicked the main isolating switch and cut off the power to the entire restaurant. Ironically, her initial fear was whether she would be sacked due to the hundreds of dollars' worth of food that would end up defrosted as a result, rather than focusing on the dire consequences she was about to face. As the restaurant plunged into darkness, the chosen ones knew it was make or break time.

CHAPTER 28

Angela lay on a luxurious purple satin coverlet in the hotel suite of her latest conquest. She was recovering from a marathon sex session with Kevin Cunningham, one of Bill's biggest business rivals. Bill thought that Angela was an innocent little intern who was exclusive to him, but he had got it all wrong. Angela was a bigger player than both of them put together. She had them fooled with her girlie voice and innocent giggle. *Hell, I even went as far as pretending to be shy when stripping for tonight's ugly beast.* It was all worth it, though. In the lead up to their sexual encounter, she'd looked at some Gucci earrings online with a quivering lip and tears in her eyes. Angela told Kevin in a sad voice how it was her dream to own a pair of these earrings at least once in her lifetime but couldn't afford them on a lowly intern salary. Angela had used this line a few times on her unsuspecting prey and as a result had several pairs of designer earrings already. She deliberately made a show of exiting the Gucci website on her mobile phone, with downcast eyes. Kevin fell for it hook, line and sinker and immediately ordered the earrings for her with a few quick clicks on his laptop.

Angela's euphoria was contagious and after flinging her arms around Kevin, her eyes shiny with fake appreciative tears, she gave him the ride of his life in addition to a token blow job. Angela grinned as she glanced at his Mastercard lying on the bedside table. The thought of tonight's win made her smile and she gave her magnificent lithe body a languid post-sex stretch, her long graceful limbs in a star shape on the bed. Kevin lay beside her, smoking a cigarette, a smug postcoital glow on his droopy jowly face.

The news was on the TV in the background and they caught the essence of the siege situation in the city, but given that both of them were too self-absorbed to care about anyone else, they didn't pay much attention. They both remained blissfully unaware of the predicament Bill was in. Ironically, that was the precise moment Bill had convinced himself that Angela would be the one to raise the alarm on his behalf. He pictured her to be out of her mind with worry, begging police to save her sugar daddy. Maybe she would realise in that moment that she was in love with him and would want to scratch Levi's eyes out for daring to dine with him. Bill had always been delusional but the knock to the head seemed to have exacerbated this.

CHAPTER 29

Behind the scenes, the tactical commander was weighing up the legal implications of shooting the gunman. The sniper had a good view of him at this point and could take him out at any time. No one in a position of authority seemed able to make a definitive decision on this and it was becoming increasingly embarrassing as the whole world watched on with avid interest.

The sniper was on edge and was beginning to feel slightly delirious. In accordance with current legislation, police believed that taking a shot was only acceptable if the hostages were in imminent danger.

Whilst some would argue they had been in danger right from the start, others would argue that whilst they were bargaining with the gunman, it would be unethical to shoot him despite the fact that he had already shot three people. It was absurd, and if the general public knew how undecisive those in high positions were being, they would be suitably outraged. The sniper was also concerned about getting a clear shot through the glass window of the restaurant. There were no guarantees that the shot would be successful, and if he failed to hit his target, then the gunman would be likely to kill the remaining hostages. Everything seemed like a catch-22 with no concrete solution in sight.

·· • ● • ··

Levi began to see her life flash in front of her. How the hell had she ended up in such a surreal situation? Her thoughts were becoming erratic and incredibly distressing, so she began disassociating from the siege as a coping mechanism. *If I close my eyes, it will all go away and won't really be happening. I'm going to think nice thoughts about happier times.* Levi began to relive her wedding day to Ben in great detail. She was there in the luxury hotel suite with her bridesmaids, Jenny and Clara. They were carefully dressing her like she was some sort of delicate princess. Every detail was perfect. Her cream lace bodice was boned and accentuated her tiny waist to perfection. As her girlfriends laced her into the bodice from the back, she marvelled at how incredibly lucky she was to be marrying the man of her dreams and that their families had the collective budget to give them the wedding they truly desired. When she carefully rolled on her fine lace silk stockings, she'd smiled at the thought of Ben's desire when he unhooked them from her suspender belt later that night. When she'd stepped daintily into her simple strapless champagne coloured silk wedding dress, she felt overcome with emotion. She kept dabbing at her eyes with a tissue in an attempt not to spoil her professional bridal make-up. But when Jenny carefully placed her late grandmother's pearls around her neck, she'd let out a little sob.

Nana May had been a wonderful lady, so generous and giving but also could have won the cheekiest old lady record in the *Guinness World Records* if she'd wanted. Once, Nana May had told Levi's previous boyfriend his aftershave smelled like sewage. Needless to say, he hadn't engaged with her much after that. In hindsight, it was her way of subtly letting Levi know she hadn't approved of him. Nana May was never rude to Ben and that was when Levi had realised he was the one for her. Levi was surprised to realise with a jolt just how much Nana May's seal of approval mattered to her.

Sadly, not long after their engagement, Levi and Ben were at a family dinner when Nana May suddenly slumped forward onto her roast beef dinner. Levi's mum, Cathy, was distraught, and it was the first time Levi thought of her mum being someone's child. Although logically she knew Nana May was her mum's mum, she had never been able to see her strong-willed mother as someone who would ever be in a situation where she would want or need her own parents. It was startling seeing Cathy crying like a young girl for the loss of her mum and made the situation all the more heartbreaking. Frantic attempts by family members to resuscitate Nana May were futile. She had already passed away when she was gently laid on the carpet by Ben. Levi thought fondly of how Ben had desperately wanted to massage her heart and put his recently acquired first aid qualification to use, but it was to no avail. Nana May was well and truly gone.

Levi's thoughts abruptly returned to the present and her mind went straight to her daughter, Charlie, while she considered the circle of life. She simply couldn't bear to think of the loss her baby girl would endure if she died here tonight. Suddenly, there it was, the reason for recalling Nana May's death became clear and finally Levi's need for survival kicked in. This wasn't just about her. It was about her daughter and husband. Levi sat up straight, her heart pounding, her eyes on stalks. Ben and Charlie needed her to survive this ordeal. Finally, the adrenaline kicked in and she was ready to fight.

CHAPTER 30

Friday 17 May 2019, 8.30pm

As the restaurant plunged into darkness, Farzad realised he had been duped by the scrawny little Indian witch. Despite his weak state, he roared an animalistic sound as rage overtook him. He sat up, panting, his legs parted, gun poised, his eyes desperately trying to adjust to the dark. Regina, who had been playing dead near his feet, suddenly rolled over with a swift move and kicked the gun straight out of Farzad's hands and well out of reach. His badly aimed earlier shot had only skimmed her left breast, and while she was in pain, he had not managed to fatally wound her as everyone first suspected. Regina had used it to her advantage and played dead so she could make a comeback when the gunman was least expecting it. She whooped with glee at successfully disarming him and was now back on her feet in full attack stance.

Paul had been careful to take stock of his surroundings and map out where everything and everybody was in his mind from the offset of the siege. He envisioned early on that cutting off the electricity would be their only solution. Jagriti knew the layout of the restaurant well and this also gave her an advantage when fumbling around in the dark. In contrast, Jacob was walking around with his arms outstretched trying to locate Paul. He jumped when the older man grabbed his upper arm from behind and hissed in a low voice, 'Shh, we need to take him down. I'm gonna try and get my hands on the gun and you need to sit on him and pin his arms to the floor till we get help. Can you do that?'

Jacob nodded in the dark and whispered, 'Yes, mate, I will do my best, let's go!' Meanwhile, Jagriti was slowly edging her way back to the front of house and wondering where everyone else's heads were at. It was strangely quiet. No one wanted to speak in case it identified exactly where they were at that moment. It felt like a game of cat and mouse. The hostages' eyes were starting to adjust to the small amount of light filtering through from the street lamps outside.

Paul palm-slapped his head. *What a dick I am – I have my phone and can use the torch.* He quickly snatched it out of his back pocket and held it up cautiously. He pointed the torch in the direction of the sound of a commotion. The sight he saw as his eyes followed the bright line of light was unexpected but welcome. Regina's rather large behind was firmly plonked on Farzad's chest, evidently suffocating him. His limbs were flailing wildly and his head was vigorously moving from side to side. Farzad managed to give her a few heavy blows but she looked completely unperturbed. It was a bizarre sight indeed. While Paul's phone torch briefly illuminated the room, Jagriti quickly spotted the gun on the floor and ran over to grab it. It was just in time as Farzad managed to wriggle free from under Regina while they battled on the floor. Jacob suddenly leapt on top of Farzad and straddled him, allowing Regina to roll off and free herself briefly while Jagriti swiftly pointed the gun in Farzad's face.

Farzad stared up at her in disbelief, his eyes cold and hard. He thought he must be hallucinating. The Indian girl was pointing his gun at him in the dark and the meathead boy was sitting on top of him. Had the American lady he killed earlier really been sitting on him too? *I'm losing my mind and my plan has gone to shit. I must have snorted too much cocaine. I should have killed the whole lot of them when I had the chance.*

Paul immediately took over as the spokesperson for the group. He would rather be the one pointing the gun and have Jagriti continue talking with the negotiator. As it was, he was just grateful that they had the upper hand at all. He couldn't help but give a wry smile that the American lady was alive and clearly possessed balls of steel. Paul's mobile phone rang before he had the chance to grab Jagriti's, which had the hotline number for the negotiator stored on it. It would seem the police weren't completely useless given that they appeared to know to ring Paul. It was a step in the right direction and gave him a small sense of comfort that despite their ominous silence for long periods, the police seemed to be watching what was unfolding and were one step ahead.

Paul answered his mobile phone, his eyes glued to Jacob and Regina, who were now *both* sitting on top of Farzad while his giant frame squirmed like a fish underneath them. Jagriti did not appear to waver and she continued pointing the gun at Farzad, a look of steely determination on her young face.

Paul confirmed the latest turn of events to the negotiator, his shoulders sagging with relief when he realised he was reiterating what police already knew. This meant they were definitely monitoring their every move. Paul followed the instructions to put the power back on in the restaurant and finally started to feel hope that they were all going to be okay. Like the others, his throat was horribly parched, his eyes were hot and dry, and it felt like he had been in the restaurant for days rather than hours. Talking of which, time was of the essence. It was now 8.30pm, only fifteen minutes from the gunman's next deadline. *Why am I worried about that?* The police would take over now and they were all going to be free. Although this was a logical train of thought, Paul's gut instinct was saying, *I don't think so mate, it's nowhere near over.*

Paul was asked to put the phone on speaker for the benefit of the others once the lights were back on in the restaurant. A deep, assertive voice came down the line. 'Okay, guys, this is Sergeant Leonard Smythe, I want you to listen carefully to what we want you to do. Police have confirmed your identities and that of the gunman. We are going to have special officers escort you out one by one and police will take over with managing the gunman. Do only as directed and in the order that you have been instructed. Officers will enter the restaurant through the main entrance in due course. Paul, if you could also unlock the door, it will save us breaking in. Do you understand?' Paul nodded whilst replying yes. He grabbed the restaurant keys from the breadbasket and swiftly unlocked the main entrance to the restaurant.

Collectively, the hostages slowly nodded that they understood the instructions, knowing they could be seen by the officers outside. Farzad continued writhing on the floor and for a few seconds he felt a sense of defeat as he heard with his own ears that police intended to storm in and take control. *Over my dead body! It's mind over matter! Focus, focus, focus!* Farzad thought back to all he endured and survived growing up in Iran. Some children had perished living in the same conditions as him, but he'd soldiered on! There was a reason for that, and *nothing* must stop him from achieving his mission tonight.

· · • ● • · ·

The hostages allowed themselves to feel slightly less guarded, knowing that it was all about to be over, subconsciously allowing relief to flood their bodies and take over from the previous fight or flight mode. Farzad sensed this and decided to seize the moment. *Carpe diem!* In a split second, he summoned up a brute strength he had no idea he was capable of. In his mind he was the Incredible Hulk. He mirrored this by letting out an almighty roar, and with supreme effort, he bucked his body upwards and flung Regina and Jacob off him. As he freed himself and sprung unsteadily to his feet, he marvelled at his superhuman strength despite the blood loss he'd endured.

It all seemed to happen in slow motion. Jagriti froze and found she was unable to fire the gun at Farzad. She continued to aim the gun at him with a blank expression on her face. Although she knew in that instant it was her life or his, her fingers would not budge on the trigger. Jagriti became aware of the surrounding commotion as everyone screamed at her, 'SHOOT

HIM! SHOOT HIM!' But still she stood rooted to the spot, frozen with terror. Shock had finally kicked in and her brain was simply not cooperating with the task at hand. Jacob and Regina scrambled to their feet and Paul advanced on Jagriti in an attempt to get the gun from her. Bill and Levi cowered on the spot. At the same time that armed police slowly edged their way into the restaurant, Farzad picked up a chair and flew at Jagriti, smashing it hard over her head. She slithered down to the floor, dropping the gun clumsily as she fell.

CHAPTER 31

Friday 17 May 2019, 8.40pm

Farzad's goal of world fame had been achieved and a close-up, sinister looking image of him taken by a journalist was doing the rounds on the internet and various social media platforms. Despite police being cagey about confirming who the hostages were at the early stages, friends and family of the captives had leaked all there was to know. Eerie posts were appearing in droves on the Facebook pages of Jacob, Regina, Jagriti, Levi and Paul. Messages of love and support flooded in, but there was only silence in return. Bill was the only one who did not have a social media account, which was probably just as well given that no one was overly concerned for his welfare or actively seeking an update on his well-being.

Serious-looking news readers on every TV channel provided regular updates, yet their segments only served to make viewers increasingly frustrated and anxious, given that little seemed to change with each report.

· · ● ● ● · ·

As Jagriti fell, police immediately aimed their guns directly at Farzad and instructed him to stay exactly where he was and place his hands in the air. He did not appear to register this command and kept his hands near his waist instead. 'HANDS UP, NOW!' commanded the police officers in unison, their weapons poised, ready to shoot. The officers were ominous in their dark combat gear, their faces covered. Jacob thought how much it looked like a scene in a crime thriller. He could not help but admire the brave officers holding their heavy guns in the aim-to-fire position. It was still their intention to get the hostages out so that only Farzad and police remained. This plan had not changed with this new turn of events. Just as the plan of action was about to commence, Farzad took a chance, and in one swift movement he snatched a hand grenade from inside his underpants and held it aloft. There was a collective gasp, followed by a stunned silence. The gunman had never mentioned explosives at any time up to now and the search of his house had not uncovered anything to indicate he was likely to be carrying any. Once again, police would later be criticised for not being mind-readers and for not shooting Farzad in the split second he'd put his hand down his pants.

With renewed confidence, Farzad held the grenade up high to indicate it still had the pin intact. He was back in business. 'I think you will find I'm calling the shots around here,' he announced proudly. He was a sinister sight, with his heavily blood-stained clothes, protruding red-veined eyeballs and sweaty face. He held the grenade in his left hand and put his thumb and forefinger of his right hand next to the pin, indicating his intention to pull it. Baring his teeth, he snarled, 'Bye-bye police! You have ten seconds to get the fuck out or we all die together!' The armed police wavered uncertainly. It was so tempting to take this prick out right now. There was every chance the grenade's detonating mechanism wasn't functional, but they knew they could not take the risk and jeopardise everyone's lives.

There was an ominous silence for a few seconds, which was broken by their tactical commander, whose voice crackled into life via the police radios. 'Do what he says and back out slowly.' With a sense of defeat, the officers retreated and the hostages could feel their blood run cold once more.

CHAPTER 32

Farzad felt different this morning. He woke up with the thought that today was the first day of the rest of his life, whatever that meant. He surmised that perhaps today was actually the last day of his life. As usual, his thoughts were jumbled and incoherent, but he knew intuitively that it would definitely be one or the other. He rubbed his protruding eyes while he tried to make sense of it all. He decided that either radical change would occur today as the result of the Chosen Seven supporting him in his quest to make the world sit up and take notice – or it would end badly and he wouldn't care because he would have checked out of planet Earth forever. Either concept was exciting beyond belief.

Farzad felt motivated by the thought of being a martyr in his role as an Islamic extremist. If he was going to be authentic about his mission, he would need to believe wholeheartedly in the value of death over life. Was he prepared to die for his faith in the name of Allah? It would mean an immediate ascent to Heaven and the beginning of life in paradise with access to seventy-two virgins! He would have a much better existence there than here on Earth. A smile played on his lips and he reassured himself of his capabilities.

Farzad carefully planned his outfit. He needed to have light casual clothes on that would not weigh him down or make him sweat too much. He would wear his recently acquired bulletproof vest to give him the upper hand. He was amazed that no one had discovered how he'd managed to sneak it into his possession. He considered how he would choose his hostages to form the chosen ones.

So far, every time he had been pumped up and ready to execute his plan, he would look around at the potential candidates in the vicinity and end up bitterly disappointed. He'd stupidly wasted money on a trip to Bali after being convinced the chosen ones would congregate there but it was not meant to be.

The chosen ones would stand out to him due to their exceptional physical or mental traits and he would know he was on the right track. Something would strike him as being intriguing about each of them and he would instinctively know to choose them. He would explain how they were privileged to be chosen and when Allah helped him to convey what they needed to hear, they would each be enriched by his teachings and embrace their newfound knowledge. If they chose not to be on board with him, they would be sorry and most definitely pay the price.

Farzad needed captives for leverage, because on his own, he would make little impact. The truth was that no one would particularly care about his welfare. He was not about to have a pity party about that. But everyone would care about six innocent people caught up in his web of atrocities.

The Australian traitors would be held accountable. The politicians would soon be sorry when he wiped the smug smiles of their faces. The prime minister would finally have to do the job he was paid to do, and more importantly, he would have no choice but to do the right thing and honour Allah.

Although the West partnered with his home country Iran to destroy the Islamic State, it would seem that the masses had forgotten an important fact: one of Iran's highest-ranking terrorists had played a big part in founding Al-Qaeda. The latest article Farzad was reading cited, 'While the Islamic State was born out of Osama bin Laden's global jihad against the West, many overlook the importance of another player in the equation, and that is Iran.'

Farzad stared at the words on his screen, a fierce expression on his face.

It was time to get off his face to take him to a higher plane. But first he needed sustenance. He ate the two large pizzas he'd ordered the night before that were lying next to his bed. He'd fallen asleep after receiving the delivery and now he enjoyed them cold despite the congealed cheese and slippery halal pepperoni that had left large greasy circles on the inner lid of the takeaway box. He ate greedily and slurped a cup of cold tea with curdled milk between mouthfuls. Randomly, he decided to clip his filthy nails and floss his teeth. He stood staring into the bathroom mirror for several minutes.

I don't know who I am, he thought. He nodded at his reflection and said aloud, 'But tonight I will find out, that is a given.'

Farzad looked around at his rental property. The navy blue sofa was second-hand and torn, with foam coming out of the well-worn areas. His furniture was mainly mismatched Salvation Army donations that he'd bought for next to nothing. The only thing Farzad invested in was his drug habit. He expertly cut, then laid out, four lines of cocaine on his glass-topped table, then snorted them in quick succession.

It did not take long before he felt the familiar rush of euphoria and invincibility. The downside was that he knew the effects also had a tendency to make him paranoid, unpredictable and aggressive…

Before long, he began to hallucinate. His dearly departed brother, Basir, appeared before him, surrounded in a kaleidoscope of bright swirling colours and patterns. Basir was levitating towards the ceiling.

He spoke sternly to Farzad and pointed an exceptionally long, bony finger at him. 'You are a fool, brother! Stop acting crazy or you will be joining me before the evening is over!' Farzad let out a deranged laugh and swiped at the air above him. He desperately wanted to connect physically with his brother, but his hands went straight through him, despite his convincing three-dimensional image. Farzad could see a pulse throbbing in his brother's neck; he was really there! He refused to believe he was on a drug trip.

'Come back, Basir! Join me back on Earth! Help me pick the chosen ones!' But Basir merely laughed at him and turned into an ugly ghoul with no eyes in its sockets, then vanished back into thin air.

Several hours later, Farzad headed for the city. His feet would take him where he needed to go. The people who would end up at his mercy would literally be in the wrong place at the wrong time. Did fate really exist – or were they just unlucky? He bellowed an insane sounding laugh while the excitement built. He carried a large black hold-all bag with his secretly acquired sawn-off shotgun over his shoulder. He casually sauntered into the city centre as though he was a normal citizen like the rest of the bores around the place.

He knew that after tonight, all the CCTV footage he appeared on would be carefully examined. Some sucker would trawl through hours of pointless footage to analyse his every move, one painstaking still at a time. How boring! How pathetic! It was hilarious that the police would have to go to so much time and trouble to examine how his day had panned out. What would it achieve when they pieced together his last movements before taking his hostages? Nothing! He never could get his head around the mechanics of police investigations. Crime dramas always baffled him. Maybe it was because he was taking the wrong angle. He would watch it rooting for the bad guy and not the other way around. His sense of justice was significantly different to the clowns brought up in the West. Now they were in for a rude shock when he welcomed them into his reality.

He turned a corner and there it was. A restaurant named Alessandro's Cucina. It had a striking rust-coloured frontage with sculpted potted plants on either side of the doorway. The enormous floor-to-ceiling windows meant you could clearly see the warm and cosy interior from outside, making it inviting to anyone passing by. ALESSANDRO'S CUCINA was displayed in large white letters above the entrance and potted flower baskets hung from underneath the sign.

Farzad knew that precision was everything and time was of the essence. He had to come across the right venue just before 6.00pm and was beginning to wonder when the hell it would jump out at him. His faith had paid off, and here it was in all its glory. The fine hairs on his body were standing on end and he experienced a flurry of goose bumps and butterflies all at once. The venue was utterly perfect. His blood and sinews told him it was so.

When Farzad entered Alessandro's Cucina, he noted a muscular, cocky-looking young man standing to one side of the counter, looking impatient. Then he spotted a demure Indian waitress talking to a handsome middle-aged tradesman.

Farzad was buzzing. He looked around and saw the staff going about their business. Not for much longer! He noted a happy looking middle-aged couple with a tower of sandwiches and cupcakes on their table. Suddenly, he was filled with hatred. He could not stand watching joyous moments, especially when it involved people interacting with each other in a loving way. His stomach lurched and heaved. The couple made him feel ill, so he averted his gaze and continued to scan the restaurant.

He noted another couple. The woman looked miserable and her body language suggested she'd rather be anywhere but there. Now that was more like it – closer to most people's miserable reality. He curtly nodded his approval while his eyes continued to travel the parameters of his chosen venue. He briefly noted a large dark-skinned woman sitting alone, but she was yet to intrigue him.

It was 6.00pm on the dot. It was time to take charge.

CHAPTER 33

As Paula drove home after having her hair done, she felt unsure about Wilfred's choice of hairstyle and couldn't help but think it was a bit too trendy for her. He'd ended up talking her into paying extra for balayage and she was now sporting pink tips on the ends of her hair. As she indicated to turn right into her street, she inwardly admitted with a resigned feeling that she'd been ripped off. She was a tad too old to pull this style off and was kicking herself for not being more assertive when doubt had first crept in. She'd peered at an image in a magazine that Wilfred waved excitedly in her face and ended up being swept away by his convincing theory on the best hair colours to complement her skin tone. It certainly wasn't anything like what she'd asked for initially.

Paula reminded herself that there was a siege going on in her own city right under her nose and therefore it was somewhat petty to be worried about her stupid hair. She was concerned that she didn't feel at all upset about Bill's predicament. She knew she was a nice person, so why was she unable to feel anything about him being held captive? *Because it's the karma he deserves after he treated me like a captive during our marriage!*

Paula felt compelled to watch the news. It was hard not to, given that it was being covered on every TV channel and was plastered all over social media. Being an empathetic person, she could not help but feel sad and afraid about what was going on for those poor hostages. Like most decent people, she hoped for a good outcome for those who were still alive. But still, the care factor she felt obliged to feel about Bill's welfare was just not forthcoming. Paula reflected back to when she first met Bill. She'd thought he was charming initially and put his other failed marriages down to sheer bad luck. One could not always assume it was the fault of the man, after all. Now she wished she had contacted his ex-wives to get the lowdown on why their marriages ended. At first Bill had wined and dined her, splashed his cash and taken her to some exotic places where he'd bought her fine things. While these things were enjoyable, they were ironically not the be all and end all for Paula. She'd wanted love, security and someone close in her life to simply just be there for her.

Bill had persuaded her to get married after a short courtship. He convinced her it was because they weren't getting any younger, so why waste any time?

Swept along with the romance of it all, Paula had agreed. She'd been widowed fifteen years prior, and it was time for some happiness in her life. The minute they were married, everything changed. Bill became patronising, moody, controlling and constantly put her down in front of others. He monitored her spending like a hawk despite his wealth and laughed in her face when she tried to have input into decorating the house with some of her own personal touches. The term 'control freak' was an understatement when it came to describing Bill.

Bill started staying out late, travelling frequently with work, and generally avoiding spending time with her. It was all a big game to him. He'd subconsciously based his relationships on the analogy his father used with regards to women when he was young. His advice to fifteen-year-old Bill was, 'It's a lot like fishing, son, you prove you can snare them, see how long they struggle in the net and then either chuck them back into the ocean or callously watch them struggle till they give up on life.' He'd laughed his wicked laugh and Bill had looked up at his father with uncertainty, but all these years later, he'd become a carbon copy of his dad. Bill had treated all of his wives this way and never participated much in his children's lives when they were growing up. He'd taken great pride in putting them down and belittling them at every opportunity. It was little wonder that when they reached adulthood, they'd all cut him off completely.

CHAPTER 34

Friday 17 May 2019 8.45pm

Following the blow to her head, Jagriti suffered a traumatic brain injury and immediately lost consciousness. Her chances of survival were dependent on how long she lay there, untreated. Her parents sobbed when they were taken to a separate quiet room to be informed of the attack on their daughter. Wringing their hands helplessly, they begged over and over that the gunman be contained and shot and an end put to this madness so their daughter could get the medical treatment she so badly needed. Realising their requests were futile, Keerti eventually accepted the offer to lie down on a makeshift bed and take strong sedatives from the nearby medics. Rahul refused any treatment and sat on the floor next to his wife with his arms around his knees, rocking silently with tears streaming down his face. He muttered an Indian prayer over and over while he wept. *Please God, if you let Jagriti live, I will drop the arranged marriage idea. I will listen to her and respect her wish to live like Western people do. I will stop being opinionated and forceful and let her choose her own husband.*

As Keerti drifted off into a troubled, drug-induced sleep, her subconscious took her back to a happier time. *Keerti was at the park with Jagriti, who was four years old. She had dressed her daughter in a traditional outfit of gold and purple silk pants with a matching sari. Keerti marvelled at how cute and smart her daughter looked with her long black plait bouncing playfully off her back while she ran around trying out the different park equipment. 'Can I take my sari off, Mummy?' Jagriti appeared at the bench Keerti was sitting on, her face flushed, her large brown eyes round and happy. Jagriti tugged impatiently at the sari; it wasn't practical to wear while navigating the play equipment. Keerti hesitated. She was feeling conflicted. Now that they lived in Australia, she wanted to be more like the locals and not be so uptight about following traditional Indian customs, but Rahul was rather set in his ways and would not approve of Jagriti's request. Keerti was all about compromise when it came to parenting. She thought it absurd that their child could not simply take the sari off to play and then resume wearing it afterwards. After all, they knew plenty of Indian families in Australia who maintained certain important customs but allowed themselves to be more relaxed with others. Keerti also considered that in order to allow their only daughter to fit in, she would have to adopt the 'when in Rome, do as the Romans do' attitude. This was the start of many similar requests from Jagriti to 'break the rules', and each time, Keerti would secretly disobey Rahul's orders and allow Jagriti to make her own choices.*

Given that she herself had an arranged marriage and was expected to be an obedient wife, Keerti secretly wanted Jagriti to have a little more freedom than she had. Keerti was lucky that she had learned to genuinely love Rahul, but she had not liked him on first sight. Even now, there were certain things he did that she tolerated only because she was conditioned to do so. Keerti desperately wanted Jagriti to keep her quiet determination and be able to make her own life decisions so that she would not suffer the same difficulties.

· · • ● • · ·

Rahul was a doctor and when it became obvious as Jagriti grew up that she was also advanced in maths and sciences, he insisted she follow suit. Jagriti was happy to study nursing but did not want to be a doctor. This caused a family feud for over a year. Finally, Rahul had to accept his daughter would not obey him and their relationship remained strained.

One day, he said to Keerti, 'I do not understand why Jagriti defies me or why she thinks it is okay to do so.' He paused, looking at Keerti accusingly. 'I sometimes think that you have taught her not to respect me. I hope this is never proven to be true.'

Keerti patted his leg, and said, 'It is your imagination, dear, her strong will is all her own doing.' But as she uttered the words, she smiled on the inside, knowing her daughter was making life choices that she never could.

'Well, she will be marrying Deepak as planned and I forbid her to think otherwise!' Rahul barked, his glasses perched halfway down his nose while he peered at his wife in his usual pompous manner. Keerti did not answer her husband. She had become good at that. He thought it was her way of meekly agreeing, but in truth she was being avoidant. She stood up and began preparing some pakoras with her special homemade mango chutney. Rahul would soon be hungry.

As these memories bubbled to the surface of Keerti's subconscious, feelings of guilt ensued. Was she being punished for encouraging Jagriti to stand up for herself? Was that why her daughter was in trouble now, because she dared to challenge the gunman? Keerti's eyes flickered. Her face looked sad and troubled while she slept. Meanwhile, Rahul had not stopped rocking; he was on the verge of a breakdown. He was a doctor and should be in there treating his daughter, but if he entered the restaurant, he may not come out alive.

CHAPTER 35

Friday 17 May 2019, 8.50pm

Farzad staggered into the centre of the room, the grenade held up high. He could hear a police helicopter above the restaurant and reminded himself with a sense of satisfaction that half of the South Australian police force were camped right outside with the TV news crews and were watching his every move. He had the urge to sing, 'Remember my name, fame! I'm gonna live forever, I'm gonna learn how to fly, high!' The hostages' faces were grim, the pits of their stomachs knotted with cold fear. Farzad's eyes glittered dangerously and had developed a hollow look. He continued to stare at them with stoned-looking eyes.

'See what you made me do you dumb fuckers?' he boasted triumphantly. His eyes swept over his captives. *The chosen ones are not so cocky now, are they?* Feeling a fresh sense of fury at how they had tried to overcome him, Farzad snarled, baring his teeth, while he contemplated his next move. *So much for the chosen ones being brainwashed by me. Perhaps I have not chosen them wisely after all.* The energy in the room had quickly changed from determination and hope to the resigned fact that they'd missed their chance of escape, lost the trust of their captor and were becoming less likely to live with every minute.

The current footage being captured by the TV crews outside was increasingly disturbing. The chosen ones looked dishevelled, despondent and weak. Their movements were becoming slower, their faces dragged downwards with terror and despair. Their body language indicated they felt defeated. The main cameraman had to look away for a few seconds, he had never filmed anything as sinister and harrowing as this. His anger was growing along with the police, paramedics, media and the rest of the nation.

Farzad was furious with Jagriti. He'd trusted her despite his hatred of women and she had let him down *kose naneh!* He looked across at her slumped body, which was awkwardly wrapped around the chair he had smashed over her head, and hoped she was dead. He had never met a woman worthy of trust in his life so why had he thought she would be any different? She was clearly bewitched and had cast some sort of spell over him. While in his right mind he would never have trusted her, not with his superior intelligence. *What did she do to me? Does she study witch craft?*

As he contemplated how long he would be under Jagriti's curse, Farzad considered grimly that the police had not come through with his request to talk with the prime minister and he'd lost track of time. It was probably close to the time he should kill someone else, but then again if the Indian girl was dead then she would count as the next one. It was all becoming too confusing. Farzad growled while he contemplated that both the American woman and the Indian girl had got in the way of his plans. He was superstitious about sticking to one shooting per hour, but he wasn't sure whether Allah would think his attack on Regina and Jagriti counted or not. Nothing was unfolding the way it should be and his brain fog was getting worse. *Perhaps it is time to just fucking kill them all.* He was getting tired and, in a way, he was becoming bored with the whole thing now.

CHAPTER 36

Two weeks ago

Levi was eating lunch at her desk. It was 2.30pm and she had been at work since 7.00am. Her bladder told her she needed to pee but her brain told her she had deadlines to meet first. It was only Wednesday but definitely felt like it should be Friday. Levi loved her job, yet at the same time she knew she'd been sucked into a relentless daily grind that was not good for her health or her family life. How did one get off the hamster wheel but still pay the mortgage and bills, though? Levi was sick and tired of her social media feed offering advice from bullshit entrepreneurs who claimed that if you paid them $100 for their secret formula, you could then get out of the rat race forever and work from a laptop on an exotic beach for the rest of your life – yeah, sure. If it was that simple, everyone would be doing it. The world was full of con artists these days and if people were desperate enough, they'd fall for it.

Levi rubbed the back of her neck to try and release some of the built-up tension. She allowed herself to stare out of the window for a few seconds. People-watching was fun, especially in the city where interesting characters walked the streets. Her office was on the ground floor, and as the windows were tinted, it meant she could see passers-by clearly, but they could not see her. A middle-aged man walked by, picking his nose. He flicked his thumb and forefinger in the direction of her window, oblivious to the fact he could be seen. Levi gagged on her chicken and walnut sandwich. People were so gross at times. Her attention became focused on two young women dressed smartly in corporate suits, their heels click-clacking on the pavement while their long, elegant legs moved with synchronicity. Both were carrying takeaway coffees and chatting animatedly to each other, their free hands gesturing while they spoke. One of them gave a hearty laugh as they passed by and inexplicably, Levi's eyes filled with tears. She stared at their retreating backs. What the hell am I becoming tearful for? Am I losing my mind, am I premenstrual? *Shaking her head as though annoyed with herself, Levi turned back to insert the data into the report that Bill was expecting by 3.00pm that day.*

While she typed, a little voice niggled her subconscious. I'm envious of those girls because they looked so happy and carefree and were enjoying each other's company. They also have time to go out and get coffee! I have no friends at work and would love the luxury of having time to stretch my legs. These are the little things that make work more bearable and I have neither. I probably earn three times what they do but they are evidently much happier than me!

Just then, Levi's new executive assistant, Molly, approached her desk. Instead of offering assistance as per the expectations associated with her job role, she snapped, 'Are you anywhere near done with the report for Bill?' Molly did not present as a happy person and this reflected in her interactions with others. Yet she had a wicked sense of humour that she rarely shared and if others did get a rare glimpse of it, they were always somewhat surprised because it seemed to contradict her usual sour demeanour. Molly was a temporary staff member and was covering the position of Levi's previous executive assistant, Samara, who was on maternity leave for twelve months.

Given that Levi was in a position of authority, she could get rid of Molly tomorrow if she wanted to. She could simply ring the agency and say, 'Thanks but no thanks, tell her not to bother coming back!' The reality was, however, that Levi simply did not have the energy to hire someone else when she was so damn busy. Levi tried to see the good in people and did note that Molly was pretty efficient at managing her diary and making sure things went to schedule when she applied herself. The problem was that she was inconsistent. One minute she would seem extremely capable and the next minute she would exude the air of someone who could not give a rat's ass about doing a good job. Hiring someone else to do the job would only mean wasting more of her precious time training them, because at the end of the day, she was the only one who could determine how things should be run in her own office.

Irritated, but trying not to give her power away by overreacting, Levi looked up and considered Molly coolly. The words of the facilitator at the course on managing conflict in the workplace she'd recently attended came flooding back to her: 'With difficult employees, you need to learn to respond versus react. Don't give your power away by having an emotional reaction because this gives them the upper hand.' Levi kept her voice even, and responded, 'Bill will be the first to know when the report is complete. It's not your concern.'

Molly stared back, an unfriendly expression on her face. 'You need anything?' she enquired brusquely with a look that said, 'I hope not because I've no intention of following through.'

Levi looked at her thoughtfully. Maybe she should make more of an effort to win Molly over. 'Actually, there is something. How do you fancy running over to Alessandro's Cucina and grabbing us a couple of takeaway coffees? I don't know about you, but I'd love one and rarely get the chance. The coffee options in the office are just not the same as a barista-made one – right? My treat if you are happy to go and grab them for us?'

Molly looked somewhat put out, and there was an awkward silence. Levi didn't make it easy for her and stared back at her, awaiting her response. Her forehead creased in frustration, as she thought, it's not like I asked her to clean dog shit off my shoe for Christ sake, it's a simple request and I'm shouting her a coffee too! What the hell is this woman's problem?

Realising she didn't have a suitable excuse not to do what Levi requested, Molly asked somewhat huffily what kind of coffee Levi wanted. Levi smiled gratefully. 'A medium almond milk cappuccino, no sugar please and whatever you are having – thanks Molly!' Levi handed Molly a $50 note and averted her attention back to the work looming on her screen. Levi hoped that would do the trick. Kill her with kindness – you never truly know what's going on for people.

Not one to hold a grudge, Levi was optimistic about Molly improving her current attitude.

Molly rolled her eyes when she left the building to get the coffees. She hated being a temp and although Levi was more bearable than some people she had worked for, she was just seriously over being someone else's bitch every day. When Molly stepped outside into the sunshine, she briefly considered that she had never done anything about changing her current circumstances. Molly had previously turned down training opportunities, refused to enrol in any tertiary study and never bothered to work hard enough to secure permanency anywhere. Molly always justified this by thinking that this would be next year's plan. It had been next year's plan for the last five years and that was why Molly was so unhappy. It was fine if one was happy to plod, there was nothing wrong with that at all; after all, the world needed plodders as well as doers. It wouldn't do if people were all the same. The problem with Molly was that she knew she had skills she hadn't tapped into. She was just downright lazy and life opportunities were passing her by. Now that she was approaching her late twenties, it was time she thought about her long-term future goals. As always, her inner voice said, blah, blah blah, who needs plans?

The only person Molly felt encouraged by was her uncle Paul. But he was an electrician and seemed self-sufficient at managing his paperwork so it's wasn't like he could help her out by hiring her. Molly's conscience prickled when she realised she hadn't checked in with her uncle for a while and probably should have because he'd taken his marriage break-up rather badly. Molly was furious with her aunt Mandy and found it hard to forgive her for hurting her beloved uncle. Molly had snorted with disgust when she heard that the reason for the split was simply because Mandy had fallen out of love with Paul. Because Mandy was her aunt by marriage to her paternal uncle, Molly felt no inclination to hear her side of the story at all. Instead, she automatically sided with her blood relative. She was biased and narrow-minded, and she knew it – but cared not a jot.

Now she thought of it, the last time she'd spotted Mandy in the city, she'd noticed she looked different. Molly had been on the bus going to work and glanced out the window to make sure she was keeping track of where she was. Molly was known to indulge in excessive scrolling on social media on her phone and had been late for work as the result of missing her stop during her previous temporary contract. The agency she was registered with was notified and she'd been warned to make sure she was on time during her current twelve-month contract. Her aunt worked a couple of blocks away, so they occasionally bumped into each other, and therefore, Molly peered out of the window with equal measures of interest and surprise when she spotted Mandy striding along wearing higher heels and a shorter skirt than usual. Molly's left eyebrow raised in a questioning arch, the way it did when she was being judgemental.

Due to a busy day ahead, she'd shelved it to the back of her mind for later. But now while she deliberately took her time getting the coffees, she considered her aunt's sudden change in appearance more carefully. Maybe Mandy had a bit on the side all along. Molly's eyes narrowed angrily as her thoughts were broken by a snappy male barista with a man bun and various colourful tattoos. 'Order for Molly!' he barked in an irritated tone. It was the voice reserved for customers whose names had clearly been called more than once and whose takeaway orders were taking up precious counter space. The barista rolled his eyes in an exasperated manner and decided he would put his name down for waiter shifts in the evenings instead. He was so over the relentless stream of coffee demands that came with the day shift. He made a mental note to speak with Alan, the owner. People were ridiculous these days with their coffee addictions and the queue always seemed to be never-ending.

His next customer was an eccentric looking elderly lady with long, frizzy grey hair, orange make-up caked into her wrinkled face and red lipstick that bled badly into the smoker's lines around her mouth. He noted with disgust that she had a mini skirt on with bony, wrinkled knees poking out from under it. She smiled a brown-toothed smile at him. 'Hey sonny, I'd like a soy latte, half strength, with a shot of hazelnut syrup and a sweetener please.' She looked at him mockingly with watery blue eyes. He could swear these old retired biddies cooked up such ludicrous drink orders just to get their kicks. He could just imagine her nudging her friend and saying, 'Hey Mabel, let's see who can come up with the most convoluted drink order of all time and see if the barista can remember it!'

With his mouth set in a grim line, the barista got to work. 'Coming right up, what was your name for the order?'

The lady smirked. 'Rosetta is the name, darling,' she said, and gave him a jaunty wink. Rosetta handed over a $10 note with a bony liver-spotted hand adorned with chipped bright orange nail polish. She tried to hold his hand just a fraction too long and jutted out her sagging breasts at the same time. The barista shuddered. She could probably throw those deflated boobs over her shoulders if she wanted to. In any case, she was so barking up the wrong tree. He wasn't into GILFs, or MILFs for that matter. Tall dark and handsome dudes were all that floated his boat. Enough was enough, he was done with day shifts, the customers were all nuts and now he was being accosted by old ladies. Working nights at Alessandro's Cucina as a waiter couldn't possibly be stressful like it was during the day, could it?

In her trance-like state, Molly had not ordered the right coffee and Levi was mighty pissed off when she took her first sip at her desk. She realised straight away that her coffee had been made with full-cream milk, which she hated. Thinking that Molly messed up her order deliberately to put her off sending her out on errands, Levi made a mental note not to pursue trying to befriend her new executive assistant any further. She didn't consider it could have been a mistake – it was a simple request, after all. Molly was simply a little bitch and she was done trying with her. It was sad that her workdays always ended up so lonely. She was a nice person, so why was she stuck in such a non-supportive toxic environment? I need to stop being ungrateful, I'm in a great position for my age, well paid and already fairly senior. Levi continued typing her report but her subconscious would not let up. But am I genuinely happy? I have no friends at work, the women are bitchy, and the men are chauvinists. My boss is a moronic dickhead who tries to flirt with me. I work so hard and hardly see my husband and child. Is that what life is all about?

Later that day, Molly sat at her desk rummaging around in her oversized tote bag, trying to find her security pass. It was so annoying that staff members needed to use their security pass every time they entered and exited the building. They had to use it just to go to the loo, which in her opinion, was ridiculous. She clearly had it on her person at some point or else how would she have got in the building? Feeling exasperated at how ditsy she was becoming, she noted Levi was taking a private call in the quiet room and had left her security pass on her desk. She had a strong urge to pee, so Molly breached the agency's strict rules never to share security passes and quickly snatched up Levi's from her desk, then bolted to the toilets with it. If she was quick, the pass would be back on Levi's desk in no time and no one would be any the wiser.

Molly rushed into the staff toilets and left Levi's security pass near the sink while she slunk into the nearest cubicle. Just as she'd bolted the door closed, Leanne, the business manager, entered the toilets a few seconds later. Leanne did a quick assessment of the bathroom and going by the security pass at the sink with Levi's name and photo on it, she felt sure that it was safe to talk. Leanne entered the second cubicle and talked rapidly while she peed. 'Geez Levi, we got a real dud with that Molly temp, she walks around with her head up her arse half the time, and she is sooo rude! I bet you can't wait till Samara gets back from maternity leave!'

Molly froze and felt the blood drain from her head. Leanne was talking about her to her! She was momentarily rendered speechless and her heart started thumping uncomfortably in her chest. She could either come clean and completely embarrass Leanne or she could go along with it and use it to her own advantage at a later date. After a few seconds of deliberation, Molly realised she would be in serious trouble if Leanne found out she was breaching the agency's rules by using Levi's security pass. She was pretty sure that pretending to be someone else was against the code of conduct or some nonsense like that. Molly quickly composed herself and tried to do a sarcastic-sounding 'mm-hmm', hoping she could pass as Levi.

Leanne was now at the sink washing her hands as she answered her mobile phone. 'Oh, has he arrived already? Yep, sure, show him in, I will be right there.' Leanne clicked her phone off, fluffed up her hair and yelled, 'Chat later Levi, I have to run.' When Leanne scurried off to meet the client who'd arrived five minutes early, she considered Levi might have an upset tummy and probably wanted some privacy anyway. It was unlike her to be in the loo for so long when she was always in a rush to meet deadlines. Shrugging, Leanne smoothed down her too-tight pencil skirt and sashayed back to her office at the opposite end of the corridor.

Molly came out of the cubicle, quickly washed her hands, noted her pale, shocked face in the mirror and promptly bolted back to the office she shared with Levi. She managed to replace the security pass with seconds to spare as Levi closed the door to the quiet room behind her and returned to her desk. Molly was grateful that Levi seemed too absorbed in whatever she was working on to need her for anything else that afternoon. Molly sat in shock as she mulled over what Leanne had said. While she stared into space, it was like Leanne's words continually played on repeat in her head. It reinforced her poor self-worth, and if she'd felt shit about herself before then, she felt ten times worse now. Would Levi have agreed with Leanne if she had genuinely been in that cubicle? Leanne must have been confident enough to think so – unless she was just a prize bitch who didn't care if those on the receiving end of her nasty tirades agreed or not. Suddenly feeling more angry than upset, Molly sat up straight. That's it! This is the catalyst for change that I need! I'm not valued here so it's high time I took action and worked towards a whole new career... but not before I seek revenge on Leanne.

The following day, Leanne asked Molly to be the contact person for anyone applying for the recently advertised receptionist role because she was too busy and had been fielding calls about the position all week from applicants with queries. Given the deadline for the job was 5.00pm that day, Leanne saw no harm in Molly answering any last-minute calls. Any basic questions that further applicants may have about the role could be covered by Molly because the role only consisted of basic admin tasks. It meant she could get on with more urgent work. Molly agreed and smiled sweetly at the request. Leanne looked taken aback. She was expecting Molly to be surly and had approached her in a determined manner, ready to tell her that it was too bad if she wasn't keen on taking the task on.

Molly grinned wickedly while she thought how to get back at Leanne for bitching about her behind her back. It's payback time, bitches! Levi had *a private business meeting with her boss, Bill, so wouldn't be there to monitor Molly's incoming calls. How deliciously perfect. Molly knew she would be dismissed for what she was about to do but she was past caring and had already organised a few casual shifts at Hungry Jack's, which was closer to home and meant no more temp agency bullshit.*

The first call came in regarding the advertised receptionist position after a few minutes. Instead of answering professionally, stating the agency name, followed by her own name, Molly answered the call by talking in an exaggerated Asian accent. 'Herro?' she spoke into the receiver, repressing a giggle. The caller was caught off guard.

'Oh um, I'm calling about the receptionist position that's been advertised, is that the right number?'

Molly interrupted the caller before she could say anything further. 'Oh wess sowee, I no speekee Engrish so well.' She coughed to cover up the belly laugh gurgling up to her throat.

There was a pause while the caller tried to determine if this was a wind-up or not. Cautiously the caller continued, 'Um so yes, can you tell me more about the position, please?'

Molly sucked in her cheeks in while she considered how to reply. 'Oh wess, the poseeshon ees only for vewee vewee speshal pehson.'

Realising that this was not a professional call, the caller replied, 'If this is some kind of joke, then I'm not amused in the slightest. This is so unprofessional and...'

Molly yawned and inspected her nails. 'Vewee bowring!' she replied to the caller, who gasped in horror.

The caller retorted angrily, 'That's it! I'm reporting you to your manager and you will be found out so don't think...'

Trying to emulate Leslie Chow from the hangover movies, Molly replied, 'Toodaloo mothafokahhhh!' before slamming the phone down. She clutched her stomach and laughed solidly for three whole minutes. She realised she'd crossed the line once more and remembered why she was never made permanent in any job role. It was because she was as free as a bird! How many people could just walk away from situations they did not want to be in at work? Not many! With a self-satisfied smirk, Molly stood up, reached for her bag and vowed never to return. She almost felt bad that Levi would come back from her meeting and wonder where the hell she was, but she didn't care enough to stick around. It was time to be rude and surly at some other workplace. At least this time she'd left before she was fired. Her uncle Paul would be mad at her, but she knew he wouldn't be able to help but laugh at her latest prank although he'd undoubtedly want to shake some sense into her.

CHAPTER 37

Friday 17 May 2019, 8.46pm

Alan Harper sat with his head in his hands, feeling utterly helpless. His beloved restaurant was under siege and there was little he could do about it. Police had interviewed him and asked for plans of the restaurants layout but would not allow him to be anywhere near the scene despite his investment in the well-being of the captives. Alan was a hands-on manager, but also, being a family man, he tried to ensure he left before 6.00pm each night and would usually leave Alessandro's Cucina in the capable hands of Tim the head waiter. Unfortunately, Tim was suffering with some health issues recently and hadn't been around to keep things running smoothly for Alan.

This was exacerbating Alan's guilt because he had stupidly allowed Jagriti to cover a lot of Tim's hours recently. He had done so because he thought she was more than capable, but she was just a young girl and now he felt responsible for the predicament she was in. He'd also found out that the electrician who was due to do some work for him was also a hostage. The police were able to ascertain his identity from his van being parked nearby. If any of the other captives were regular customers, there was a good chance he knew them too. He understood the reasons police would only allow close friends and family to enter the specially designated area, but he was being kept completely on the outer and felt useless. Alan rationalised that none of this was his fault and he could not possibly have pre-empted what would happen, but all the same, his body was rigid with tension and he felt unable to function while he watched the continual news coverage that never seemed to offer any positive updates. Alan massaged his temples and thought how ironic it was that one of his daytime baristas had recently asked to swap over to evening shifts to give him a change of scene. He was sure to be counting his lucky stars that Alan hadn't got around to changing the staff roster or he'd be stuck there now with the other hostages.

Meanwhile, Molly sat biting her nails and watched the news over and over again on every channel. Somehow she hoped that one channel would say something more positive than the other, but unfortunately the coverage of the siege was pretty consistent on each one. Now she knew why her uncle Paul hadn't been returning her calls and it was giving her chills. Molly couldn't make up her mind whether to call her aunt Mandy or not. *We should be comforting each other, but did the bitch even care when she'd just left Paul in such a callous manner?* It didn't occur to Mandy that people didn't deliberately fall out of love. By her own admission, she was rather narrow-minded and didn't have the ability to see anyone else's view. It was why her relationships constantly failed and her work contracts were never renewed. It was all about her and to hell with anyone else. Paul blamed his sister, Marilyn, for spoiling her only daughter and never dishing out any consequences. She certainly hadn't been successful in teaching his niece that the world didn't revolve around her.

·· • ◉ • ··

Paul felt like he had a heartbeat pulsing in his head. It was throbbing and beating like a drum at his temples. His previous euphoria at overcoming Farzad had all but evaporated. It had been like a sick joke when he'd pulled out the hand grenade with that triumphant look on his smug face. Like the police, Paul also had his suspicions about whether the grenade was a genuine explosive but understood the officers had no choice but to retreat for fear of everyone being blown to smithereens. All the same, he was resentful of them leaving and the irrational part of him blamed the police for the predicament they were now in. He sensed the others felt much the same way. The hostages' previous expressions of fear and horror were now being replaced with angry yet resigned ones. They could not afford to give up hope, not now. Paul tried to fight off the negative talk in his head and wracked his brain to think of the positives. He was still alive; it was a start. He also still had the fork stashed in his pants but now that Farzad was waving the grenade around like some prized trophy, he was unsure of how to go about using it. So far, anyone that had tried to take on Farzad or charge at him had ended up worse for wear.

Levi was praying, her eyes rolled upwards at the ceiling. *Please give me inspiration, universe, God or whatever controls our fate in the end.* She was digging her nails into the palms of her hands so hard that they were bleeding, but she wasn't aware of this. All she could see was the faces of her husband and baby girl as though their images had been enlarged and imprinted on her brain. They needed her and she *would* return to them. It was not up for negotiation. She desperately wanted to give medical assistance to Jagriti and to cover up the bodies of the couple who'd been shot. All of a sudden, the enormity of what she had endured and witnessed so far hit her like a ton of bricks and a wave of nausea engulfed her entire body. Levi abruptly turned her head to the side to face away from the others while her stomach turned to acid and vomit erupted from her in clumps of yellow bile onto the restaurant floor.

Farzad was enraged. His childhood phobia of vomit came surging back to him as he looked over with disgust at Levi. He should kill the filthy bitch right now. Suddenly his knees buckled underneath him, and his face turned a strange shade of green. He stumbled and became unsteady on his feel while childhood memories came back to haunt him. *Fuck! I am dizzy and everything is going black. I need to man the fuck up! Who the hell passes out over someone vomiting? Focus, focus, focus!*

CHAPTER 38

Friday 17 May 2019, 8.47pm

Jacob was closest to Farzad and could see him floundering. If he staggered around like that for much longer then he would drop the grenade and they'd all be blown to pieces. He had to act and quickly.

'You don't look so well.' Jacob looked up at Farzad, feigning a concerned look. 'Can I help you to a chair?' Farzad continued to sway with the grenade in his hand, but his arm had dropped considerably and was much lower than before. He was now holding the grenade level with his shoulder rather than above his head. It was obvious to all that he might drop it at any time, either due to fatigue or intentionally. Farzad did not reply to Jacob and it appeared that he hadn't registered that he was being spoken to. His expression was blank, and he looked like he had well and truly checked out mentally. *The lights are on, but nobody is home. It's now or never*, thought Jacob.

Farzad stumbled forward. In addition to his previous injury, his severe phobia of vomit was making him seriously close to suffering a blackout. He was also coming down from his earlier cocaine hit and not feeling too flash at all. The hostages were swimming in and out of focus as blackness threatened to engulf him. Jacob's agility training came in handy and he suddenly leapt to his feet in a swift move to grab Farzad by the shoulders to stop him toppling over. His biceps were certainly being put to good use.

Farzad's eyes rolled back in his head as he fainted. He slumped heavily in Jacob's arms and there was a collective gasp of horror when his grip loosened on the grenade. It all appeared to happen in slow motion as Paul used his expert goalkeeper moves from his youth to dive down low and catch it just before it hit the ground. The question was, what the hell did he do with it now? He caught it just in the nick of time and now his heart was beating wildly as he froze on the spot. They all knew Farzad was only momentarily out of action and like the baddies in the movies, he would probably keep resurfacing when least expected. 'The fork!' Paul shouted. 'It's in my front pocket – quick! Someone grab it and do what needs to be done to disable this prick before he becomes compos mentis again!'

Regina didn't hesitate despite her earlier injury. She charged towards Paul with her nostrils flared and grabbed the fork out of his pocket as instructed. Bill chimed in, 'I don't think I can stomach this, where do we stab him exactly?'

Regina glared at him. 'Who the fuck cares where we stab him, you drip? Do you want to fucking die here, or do you want to help us rid the world of this crazy bastard?' She held the fork up in her fist menacingly, her eyes gleaming.

Bill shrank back, feeling uncertain and somewhat emasculated. Paul continued to stand as still as possible whilst holding the grenade. His nerves were frayed and he was unsure of how easily it could go off if it was real. It was safer to stay rooted to the spot until they managed to contain the gunman and let the police take over again.

Jacob let Farzad fall to the floor and was happy to watch his head hit the ground with a nasty thud. The police were watching closely and were aware time was of the essence. Just when the officers on standby were about to storm in for a second time, Regina crouched over Farzad and plunged the fork into his chest. It didn't penetrate and it slid straight out of her hands on to the floor.

'The fucker is wearing some kind of chest armour,' she yelled out in frustration. Farzad's limbs began to twitch and his eye lids were flickering.

He was coming around slowly but surely. With lightning speed and a look of sheer determination, Levi snatched up the fork and kneeled over Farzad, her eyes wide with terror. She paused, then squeezed her eyes shut tightly as she plunged the fork full force into his neck before collapsing onto the floor. She was shaking violently with her hand clamped over her mouth when she realised the fork had got stuck halfway in. She had no idea how badly she'd hurt him and felt both sick and euphoric at the same time. She started dry retching again and bile filled her mouth once more. Farzad's eyes suddenly sprung wide open, he sat up looking around wildly then became aware of the searing pain on the right side of his neck. He staggered to his feet and felt the fork with his right hand. He let out an almighty animalistic roar as he tried without success to pull it out. Blood was dripping down onto his collarbone and the hatred in his eyes made him look like a sinister character from a horror film. Finally, the police had the upper hand and had crept back in. Farzad could see the distinct red laser beam being aimed at his body and knew he would be shot at any minute. It seemed like déjà vu when he reached into the waistband of his pants just like the first time the police had entered the restaurant.

The sniper knew he could not take the chance of Farzad pulling out another explosive and made the decision to fire at him. This decision would also be highly criticised in the coroner's court because if the gunman *did* have another explosive, the sniper could potentially have blown them all up. The sniper quickly weighed up the situation and did not wait for further commands to be issued. Time was of the essence and this situation needed to reach a conclusion, and fast. Given the information that the gunman might be wearing a bulletproof vest, he had no choice but to shoot him in the head. The sniper did not have time to fully consider the pros and cons and acted on his own survival instinct when he finally took the fatal shot. Farzad felt the pain tear through his brain and he staggered backwards before crashing to the floor with a heavy thud. His final thought was that being shot felt exactly like he thought it would. A deep searing agony that would shut down his vital organs and take away his miserable existence any second. He was glad of it, he welcomed it, he wanted out of this thing they called life. His life flashed briefly before him: his childhood in Iran, the horrors he lived through, and then suddenly he was free from thinking ever again. Blackness overcame him and his life ebbed away. It was messy and gruesome as bits of Farzad's brain splattered on the cream-coloured walls, a spray of bright red blood spurting furiously from the hole in his head. Some wanted the satisfaction of watching, but others turned away, the horror being too much to bear.

· · • ⬤ • · ·

At exactly 9.00pm, the siege was over. It was the longest three hours of the hostages' lives. The bomb squad swooped in like black-suited ninjas and the grenade was quickly whisked away for safe disposal. Farzad's body was searched and no other weapons or explosives were found, much to the relief of the sniper who had made the decision to shoot.

CHAPTER 39

Friday 17 May 2019, 9.01pm

Levi slumped in a heap while relief surged through her body. She was hyperventilating but knew deep down that she would be okay. She would no doubt suffer from nightmares and Post Traumatic Stress Disorder (PTSD), but she would get the best therapy there was. She put her head between her knees and took several deep breaths to steady herself. There was a commotion as police stormed in and no one was listening to instructions anymore. It was mayhem and had become a free-for-all.

Paul and Jacob were high-fiving and exchanging manly hugs, both of them pale and ashen despite their perceived bravado. Regina did not appear to be overly affected by it all. Living in the Bronx had made her into one tough cookie. She was more worried about how dishevelled she looked. Bill was visibly shaken; he felt like he was having an out-of-body experience of some sort. He felt like a completely different man from the one who had entered the restaurant only three hours ago. He felt humble and grateful and intended to keep all his bargains with God that he'd silently made in his head whilst praying to be spared his life.

Everyone instinctively wanted to help Jagriti, but the police were adamant that only specialised paramedics could tend to her. She looked so frail and her limbs were sticking out at awkward angles. Her long black plait fanned out from the back of her head, making her look childlike and vulnerable. She was a tragic sight even for the hardened officers, who looked on at her sadly.

As the hostages were led out by police and as it became widely known that the gunman was dead, their relatives rushed towards the scene before being given permission. No one in authority had the heart to stop them and knew they would have a mighty fight on their hands if they dared to try. Orders had been issued to have the hostages thoroughly checked over in hospital, take their individual statements as soon as possible and if anyone was up to it, they could consider giving their story to the pack of journalists who were hanging around like vultures waiting to pounce on their prey.

Bill had never believed in life-defining moments or epiphanies and usually sneered at anyone who claimed to have experienced one. But the moment he was set free, he suddenly felt lost in a sea of hostages and their loved ones who were all wildly clamouring to be reunited. All around him, people were hugging and crying tears of relief or whooping with joy. People cared deeply about each other, and yet here he was, a solitary figure with no one to greet him other than police and paramedics who only wanted to check him over because they had a duty of care to do so. Bill swallowed hard and a massive lump formed in his throat. He could see Levi to his right. Her husband swept her off her feet and spun her around gleefully in a circle. He then scooped up their daughter who had just arrived with Levi's relieved-looking parents for a group hug. Bill felt invisible in that moment. He was not imagining that no one noticed him; it was a fact. He felt remorseful as he watched the loving exchanges between Levi's family members and realised with shame that he had no right to try and have his wicked way with her. She was a happily married woman. There was truly such a thing, it would seem. He vowed to apologise for his previous treatment of her and would give her the promotion she deserved based on merit rather than in exchange for sexual favours. He had a hunch Levi would have walked away from her job rather than sleep with him anyway and the reality was that she was a major asset he couldn't afford to lose.

Bill realised for the first time in his entire life that he had been unbearable towards his ex-wives and children. He cringed and thought of what they might have said at his funeral if he'd died here tonight. Would they have come? Could he blame them? Remorse was not a feeling he was familiar with, but it seemed to be radiating from his head to his toes. He vowed from this moment onwards to be a better person. He had been given a second chance at life and he meant to use it wisely this time.

Bill watched the paramedics who'd been on standby for so long rush into the restaurant to work on Jagriti, her anguished parents following close behind. Minutes later, Jagriti was on a stretcher being carefully bundled into the back of the ambulance that had been stationed outside the restaurant for the last three hours. He looked on at Keerti and Rahul, who stepped into the ambulance behind their daughter, their faces dragged down with the weight of their terror and the fear of loss. Bill had a sudden flashback of not being there for his son Liam when he'd suffered from anaphylactic shock and it weighed heavily on him now as the reality of what could have gone wrong that day finally hit him.

Bill was further sobered by the sight of officers carrying two black body bags out of the restaurant. He knew they contained the corpses of the poor unsuspecting couple who became the unfortunate victims of their captor. They had done nothing to deserve such a horrific end to their lives. Bill felt his throat constrict as he fought back the tears. He recalled how happy the couple seemed when he'd sauntered past them earlier. He vividly recalled the woman laughing at something the man said to her. They'd had an air of excitement about them. He was sure they were celebrating something. Ordinarily, Bill wouldn't give people he didn't know a second thought, but this felt so personal somehow. He realised he was grateful that he was still living. The couple would never be able to enjoy treasured moments with their family ever again. But Bill could, and Bill *would*. It was his mission to ensure this happened.

Bill looked over at Jacob, who in turn was watching the ambulance pick up speed as it left the scene. Jacob's eyes were full of fear while he silently prayed Jagriti would make it. She had been so brave and deserved to be recognised for her actions. Bill thought that this bear of a young man suddenly looked like a frightened child next to his relieved parents. The truth was that Jacob was feeling inadequate and guilty that he hadn't been able to do more to help Jagriti. He really hoped she lived and wouldn't rest until he heard how she was. Like the other chosen ones, Jacob had reflected somewhat and realised his life was superficial in many ways. Tonight had taught him about what truly mattered. It definitely wasn't all about having the perfect abdominals or biceps. Jackie always used to joke about all the women on the Titanic who'd skipped dessert in a bid to watch their waistlines but drowned when the ship sunk. 'Was it worth it? If we knew today was our last, would we be so rigid about everything? I'd rather drown with a ton of chocolate mousse in my belly than not savouring a single mouthful due to vanity!' she'd said. Jacob used to think his mother was mad, but suddenly those words of wisdom resonated with him. *We are here for a good time, not for a long time.* Being disciplined was admirable but being extreme wasn't. Jacob suddenly craved a huge bar of chocolate and was horrified to think he may never have eaten one again.

Jackie's mobile phone was being passed around so that each family member could reassure Leonie that it was truly over, and her brother would live to tell the tale. Colin joked that that they might have to buy a spiralizer so he could make zoodles at home if it meant keeping his son out of trouble.

·· • ● • ··

Mandy approached Paul cautiously. They had not seen each other for months and despite the circumstances, there was still an awkwardness between them. Both their sons were on their way and were coming straight from the airport; they'd been out of their minds with worry about their father. While Paul appreciated her checking on his welfare, he didn't want

Mandy to only be there out of pity. He was somewhat surprised when Mandy hugged him and clung onto him tightly. He sensed she wasn't going to break the hug, so he eventually pulled away gently and held her at arm's length. 'Are you okay?' they both said in unison. They both laughed, and the tension was broken. Mandy took Paul's face in her hands and placed her face close to his. Her eyes filled with tears when she spoke. 'Paul, you have every right to tell me to eff off, but I want you to know that this horrific experience has taught me how much the world needs you in it, but more importantly, how much I need you in my life.' Mandy lowered her eyes, her lips trembling. She had an awful feeling it was too late for him to forgive her for ending their marriage.

Paul lifted Mandy's chin with the underside of his forefinger and tilted her face up so that their eyes met. 'It was worth going through all of that just to make you realise that,' he said softly.

'Really?' Mandy whispered as fresh tears rolled down her face.

'Really,' smiled Paul.

Mandy felt relief wash over her but suddenly she tensed. 'Paul, I did something stupid while we were apart, I...'

Paul interrupted her and put a hand up. 'I don't want to know,' he said solemnly. Mandy looked surprised and stepped back to study his face more intently. Paul continued, 'By telling me what you've done, will it make you feel better or me? If it's going to make me feel like shit and you truly regret doing it with zero intention to do it again, then what purpose does it serve to tell me? What I don't know can't hurt me, so I don't want to know. Your need to tell me is to be rid of *your* guilt, but if you are ready to re-commit then it's yesterday's news.' Mandy shook her head in wonderment. Paul was one of a kind. It was certainly an unusual response compared to various horrible scenes her friends had experienced following their confessions of infidelity. He was one amazing man and she had been a fool to let him go. Despite what he'd just endured, he still looked damn sexy. Why had she lost sight of that? It was like seeing him through fresh eyes again and she liked what she saw. Feeling humble and grateful, she snuggled into him, her head resting on the familiar spot on his shoulder. Mandy was determined to make it up to him and was already planning to cook him a lavish dinner, plan a dirty weekend away and to buy some sexy new underwear in a bid to revamp their sex life.

Her so called friend Janet would be spewing that they were back together. Mandy knew all about her little ploy to get Paul into bed under the guise of having him undertake electrical work at her house. Janet had stupidly told the story about Paul rejecting her advances to a mutual friend Harriet over a few wines. Harriet being unable to resist gossip had passed the story on to Mandy in the guise of concern even though she was after Paul's body herself. Mandy was on to both of them and decided new beginnings were on the cards for both her marriage and her friendships.

In a sense she was strangely thankful towards Janet because the jolt of jealousy she'd felt when Harriet spilled the beans about what had happened behind her back made her realise she still had strong feelings for Paul. The fact that he had rejected Janet's advances had made her value him all the more. Paul was the best and she would *never* lose sight of this again.

CHAPTER 40

Bill was startled when he saw Regina saunter out from the restaurant. He'd momentarily forgotten all about her; how was that possible? There did not appear to be anyone there to meet her either. This gave Bill a childish sense of euphoria. Despite her minor injury, Regina had slipped into the ladies' to freshen up and reapply her lip gloss before making an appearance. After all, there would be TV crews and she needed to look mighty fine if she was going to be seen all over the world. A police officer who was doing a head count had just come looking for her and Regina had told the female officer to stop fussing and took her time while she fluffed out her hair in the mirror. After reassuring police and paramedics that she was fine, they'd assessed her left breast and noted that miraculously, she had only suffered a minor graze. Regina allowed the female paramedic to apply a light gauze dressing despite her insistence that she thought it was a big fuss about nothing.

Regina was advised like everyone else that no one could leave just yet until police had taken statements and everyone's vital signs were checked again. She rolled her eyes to indicate her disgust with how dramatic they were all being. It was most likely that all the hostages would be carted off to hospital regardless of how they said they were feeling just in case they were suffering from shock or had any unknown injuries. For now, though, everyone was just grateful that the police and paramedics were allowing them the time to just hug their loved ones and regroup.

Bill and Regina naturally gravitated towards each other, given that neither had anyone else there to greet them. Both eyed each other warily whilst at the same time feeling a strange sense of gratitude for each other's company. The old Bill would never have looked twice at a big, bold, dark-skinned lady like Regina. The old Regina would certainly not tolerate the bullshit the old Bill dished out to women. But something strange had occurred over the last few hours and they had both experienced energetic shifts in their outlook due to being subjected to a life-threatening situation.

Regina was surprised to suddenly realise that she could dig Bill in a rodeo outfit. His sandy hair and craggy face could be compared to Paul Hogan after a few drinks. *Why am I thinking about sex at a time like this? Am I that desperate? I'm sure I read somewhere that high intensity situations make people horny – is that what is happening right now? Did being in a siege situation make for a good aphrodisiac?* Regina gave a throaty chuckle whilst emitting what she hoped was a sexy aura. She stood up a little straighter to make her large bust appear more pert and smacked her freshly glossed lips together to form her trademark pout.

Bill experienced a lightbulb moment of inspiration when he realised he'd failed in his past relationships due to always picking women who never stood up to him. It was time for something different. It was time for someone who would keep him in line and not tolerate his domineering and facetious nature. He couldn't believe he was actually thinking this and perhaps he was delirious as the result of being smacked on the head and held hostage... but he was seriously thinking a woman like Regina could be the answer. He looked at her curiously. She wasn't the type he would normally go for physically or personality-wise, but he was definitely feeling a strong energetic pull to her and before he knew it, he heard himself say, 'You were so brave in there – braver than I could ever be. I admire a strong woman. Are you interested in having dinner with me sometime once we have recovered from our ordeal?'

Regina considered the question, her head tilted to one side, and she chewed thoughtfully on her thick bottom lip. Her bosom heaved and she sighed dramatically with her nostrils flared while her eyes flashed dangerously at him. She was semi-keen, but she wasn't going to make it easy for him. 'I ain't gonna lie, you came across as a bit of a wuss in there.' Regina pointed a stubby finger back towards the restaurant. The old Bill would have responded defensively to that comment. The new Bill merely nodded in agreement. Regina continued, 'You ain't my usual type but there's something aboutcha.' Her beady eyes narrowed critically. 'I don't put up with no shit though, just so you know!' Bill laughed heartily at her response. This woman was something else. She was so completely different to any other female he had ever met. She was a force to be reckoned with and he was truly shocked to realise he might enjoy the challenge of winning her over.

Bill's exes had all been subservient and his mistresses just gold diggers. Neither type had given him any real joy. Having no one there to greet him tonight had really sunk in for him and he vowed then and there to reconnect with his ex-wives and kids and do his best to maintain respectful relationships with them even if it was deemed to be too late to do so. He might even call his old man to check in with him. Bill had experienced a profound moment that made himself reflect and look within at his own behaviour. So it would seem that some good had come from his ordeal after all. Taking ownership was a new concept for Bill, but he was damn well going to do it. *Life is not a rehearsal.* Facing death did funny things to people. He'd heard this many times but only now truly understood how the intensity of such a situation made you question what mattered most in life and question your own morals and values. Both Bill and Regina were utterly amazed that they readily swapped phone numbers, both fully aware that this exchange would not have taken place prior to their recent ordeal. They were both changed people. Their first impressions of each other only a few hours ago had not been positive at all. Life really could change in an instant.

CHAPTER 41

To celebrate the end of the siege, Superintendent John Marshall went out to party with the close-knit group of officers he worked alongside. He was well aware that any officer who was able to get through a siege situation and live to tell the tale ended up having a close bond with all involved. You had to be one of the guys right in the thick of it to understand this. He knew that the police force would be hauled over the coals and criticised by the coroner, the media and the powers that be for what they *could* have or *should* have done to manage and contain the siege earlier than they had. There was rarely any praise for what they did well or for the fact that they were only human yet still put their own lives at risk in the line of duty. No matter what action police took, they were always damned if they did and damned if they didn't.

All in all, Marshall was feeling okay about the final outcome. It was unfortunate that there had been fatalities, but for the moment he would focus on the miracle that all six hostages were alive. He could live with that and was pretty happy that the worst-case scenario had not eventuated. Briony was propping up the bar with a glass of white wine in her hand. It was uncanny how watching her now felt like déjà vu from all those years ago when they were in their twenties, celebrating their respective graduations. As the night went on and their drunken colleagues started to disperse, Marshall and Briony found themselves alone in a dark booth for two. No words were spoken but they were both aware of the chemistry that had haunted them for all those years. Marshall stared at the crevice that was her deep, milky white cleavage and wondered how on earth they'd shown restraint for all these years. With lust in his eyes, he nodded at her and she nodded back. They had unfinished business to take care of. They went back to Briony's place and had sex in every position they could think of. They knew it would not be spoken of again. Marshall went home to his wife and Briony resumed her independent life. She liked it that way. But when she washed off Marshall's scent in the shower post-sex, she considered that maybe she should have snapped him up when he was available all those years ago. Marshall had been the only man to give her an orgasm. It was a secret she would take to the grave. Briony had met his skinny, flat-chested wife at several events and purposefully avoided saying anything more than a polite hello for fear of her sensing the obvious chemistry Briony had with her husband. Marshall was grateful to Briony for this and her discretion won his respect.

In her role as a police psychologist, Briony often had officers seek her out for confidential advice and therapy. When a butch-looking female officer named Tessa Peterson had recently confessed her secret love affair with Marshall's wife, she'd felt the most conflicted about keeping confidentiality as she had over the span of her entire career.

She'd tossed and turned for weeks on end about *that* little snippet of news. Briony highly doubted that Marshall had any idea of his wife's sexual preference. Eventually, she decided she had to remain professional, because she would most definitely lose her career over it if she spilled the beans. It was why Briony had felt no guilt when she finally succumbed to Marshall's probing hands again after such a long period of abstinence.

·· • ◉ • ··

The chosen ones kept in touch with each other, but only Jacob took up Regina's offer to catch up in person. Other than Bill, the others found it too harrowing to keep revisiting what happened. Jacob was intrigued by Regina's sudden fame, especially when she gained a million more Instagram followers than *he* had. That made her pretty cool, to say the least. He didn't even mind when Regina gave him shit live on air on his favourite radio station about the fact that he *used* to eat low carb pasta made from zoodles … and that if he hadn't ordered them from Alessandro's Cucina that night, he would never have been taken hostage. He had since realised that life was too short and resumed eating normal spaghetti with the rest of his nutty family.

CHAPTER 42

Six weeks later

Jagriti was well on her way to making a full recovery and like everyone else, she'd considered what was most important to her during her ordeal. She was able to sit up in her hospital bed and eat the chapatis that Keerti had secretly snuck in. The hospital food was beyond revolting; it was a wonder it didn't make patients sicker than they already were. Jagriti took Rahul's hand in hers and looked him squarely in the eyes. 'Dad, I'm not marrying Deepak and I'm not continuing with my nursing degree.' She paused, allowing her father to take in her news.

'Nonsense!' he barked, his lips pursed. 'You are delirious from the drugs you are being administered!'

Rahul knew deep down that this little speech had been coming but was unable to stop himself from reacting in his usual way. He was so used to being controlling that the words just rolled off his tongue even though he hadn't meant them to. He wanted one last shot at making Jagriti see things his way. But Rahul hadn't forgotten his bargain with God. He'd vowed to let her live her life in the way she chose if she was spared. It was imperative that he honoured that. He'd expected her to refuse to marry Deepak, but he certainly hadn't expected her to change career paths. He was struggling considerably with this concept. 'I love working in hospitality, Dad.' Jagriti gave a small smile before continuing. 'Mum has taught me to cook traditional fare and I want to apply for a business loan to open Jagriti's Indian Restaurant when I'm better. I'd like your blessing.' Keerti nodded and smiled encouragingly at her daughter. Rahul could not help but feel there had been conversations over the last few months that he had not been privy to and felt more than a little left out. His face contorted as if in pain, but when he saw how brightly Jagriti's eyes were shining with anticipation, he realised he had never seen her look so happy before. So instead of opposing her ideas, he forced himself to nod. 'Jagriti, my darling, you are alive and for that I can only be grateful. Live your life as you wish and not as I wish. You have my blessing.'

Jacob became a local hero, but he only revelled in it once he found out Jagriti was on the mend. For some reason he could not stop thinking about her. She'd had such a strong, quiet and graceful presence about her throughout their ordeal. He'd thought about how his girlfriend, Layla, would have reacted in the same situation and couldn't help but think she'd be too busy wondering if her fake eyelashes were still intact. Perhaps he was being harsh, but he realised he and Layla had both been pretty superficial in the way they went about their lives. Everything was all about how they looked, what they wore and what they ate. It all seemed dull and pointless once you'd been through something like this. Layla hadn't even flown back from Europe when she'd heard about the siege and for Jacob that was a deal-breaker.

When he told Layla over Skype that he thought they should end their relationship, he was horrified to discover she was relieved rather than upset. Apparently, there were lots of hot guys in Spain and she was too young to be tied down, hence she heartily agreed with him.

Jacob's ego was crushed further when he'd gone to visit Jagriti and surprised himself by asking her if she'd like to go out for dinner when she was feeling up to it. She'd let him down gently, saying he wasn't her type, but she would still like to be friends. *What the hell!* Prior to the siege, Jacob had honestly thought he'd have to be *everybody's* type. He was usually told several times a day that he was smoking hot on social media and he'd been brainwashed into thinking he was God's gift to women. Jackie advised Jacob that it hadn't done him any harm to be taken down a peg or two. He could certainly count on his mum to tell it how it was. Jackie *had* been a little disappointed that Jagriti had turned him down, though, because she secretly wanted an Indian friend who could cook all of her favourite curries. Not that she was making it about her or anything…

Once Jackie and Colin were over the ordeal of the last few weeks, they resumed their petty quarrels. Strangely, even though Jacob was often exasperated by them, it was this familiarity he'd secretly missed when he was wondering if he'd ever see his parents again during the siege. Admittedly, he was listening to them presently and their conversation was making him roll his eyes with exasperation, but he wouldn't have it any other way. He tuned in to his parent's latest row coming from the lounge. He could hear his mum's sarcastic tone towards his dad while he tried to talk over the top of her. 'Oh, I'm sorry, Colin, did the middle of my sentence just interrupt the beginning of yours?'

Colin came back quickly with, 'Well, if I could ever get a word in edgeways, I wouldn't have to interrupt you, would I? So, anyway, Jackie, as I was saying, I think the outfit you want to wear tonight is a bit… um… inappropriate for your age group, to be honest.'

There was a brief silence, so Jacob peered around the doorway to spy on them. It wasn't like his mum not to have an instant smart reply to his dad. He was somewhat confused to see her holding up binoculars and looking through them at nothing in particular out the window. Jacob was about to barge in and ask his mum if she'd lost her mind when Colin piped up. 'Jackie, what the hell are you doing? Is this the latest way of snooping on the neighbours?'

Standing on her tiptoes, Jackie continued to peer out the window with the binoculars up to her eyes and replied, 'I'm looking for who the hell asked your opinion on my outfit!' Then she threw herself down onto the sofa, shrieking with laughter. Sniggering at his mother, who had her right hand in a salute over her right eyebrow to mimic looking out to sea, Jacob cottoned on to the idea that she was looking for who'd asked Colin's view about her proposed outfit and the three of them howled until their faces hurt. It was great stress relief after the last few weeks.

Once they finally managed to compose themselves, Colin said, 'I have an announcement to make' and put on his best solemn face.

'Oh yeah?' replied Jackie, whilst wiping her tear-stained face.

Colin stood up and pointed to his large belly. 'I'm fat, but I identify as skinny, so I'm a translender!' Once again, the three of them erupted into whoops of laughter. Leonie came down from her room to see what all the hilarity was about and when Colin relayed the latest banter breathlessly whilst slapping his thigh, she laughed politely but then pointed at her parents with her eyes narrowed.

'Neither of you are original,' she announced. 'You think you are both so funny, but I've seen all your lame jokes already on Facebook memes.' Instead of being offended, this just made her parents laugh more. Leonie shook her head. Her family was all nuts but she'd realised just how much she loved them all when her brother's life had been in danger. Like Jacob, she was relived to resume the craziness that was their household.

·· • ● • ··

Regina was the only one who was interested in selling her story and had become something of a celebrity since she embraced the opportunity to go on several TV and radio shows to talk about her ordeal. She was making a lot of money from it and paid for Zion to fly over to Australia to meet her new lover. When Zion went to Alessandro's Cucina to take selfies outside the now world-famous restaurant, he happened to meet the barista with the man bun and tattoos who worked there. They got on like a house on fire and ended up at a gay bar where Wilfred the hair stylist was dancing on a podium in knee-high pink boots and a mink fur coat. Regina and Zion both decided they were in love with their respective new partners and with Australia in general.

Having a rich contact like Bill meant that they had someone who could sponsor them and vouch for their good character. Regina vowed to stay out of trouble until she secured permanent residency. Given that her skills were still in demand in Australia, there was every chance of obtaining an extended visa. Regina and Bill became inseparable and were delighted to discover they were both insatiable. When Regina turned up at his place dressed in a latex Wonder Woman outfit, Bill managed six marathon sex sessions in one night *without Viagra*. Bill and Regina were head over heels in love. It was a first for both of them. They decided they would get married in Las Vegas and have a tacky Elvis type ceremony. Bill did not dare mention that his lawyer had insisted he draw up a prenuptial agreement this time for fear that Regina would go crazy. Of some comfort was the fact that this feisty woman from the Bronx did not have expensive taste like his ex-wives. The only thing she indulged in was lip gloss. Her fame following the siege had also made her a fair bit of money in her own right *and* she worked at a well-paid job. He had nothing to worry about. Bill chuckled and considered maybe he should buy shares in Sephora to keep Regina happy. Securing citizenship for Regina and Zion was the next step. Bill had never felt happier.

Bill completely changed his attitude towards Levi and gave her the promotion she deserved. He suggested she work less hours so she could spend time with her husband and daughter. Due to his own regrets, he felt he could redeem himself somewhat if he could at least help someone else see their kid grow up. Levi was delighted and did not hesitate to take Bill up on his offer. Bill took tentative steps to reconnect with his elderly father and his adult children. While he wasn't welcomed with open arms, their curiosity about his ordeal slowly drew them in. Who could resist getting an inside scoop on the siege that was trending online right now? Despite her being the heroine that stabbed that gunman, Levi refused all offers to tell her story and instead sought solace in a therapist who specialised in post-traumatic stress. A few weeks later, Levi discovered she was expecting her second child and was over the moon when Bill encouraged her to take a full year of maternity pay towards the end of the pregnancy and then work from home when she was ready to resume her role. Ben and Charlie were ecstatic to have more time with Levi and Ben finally stopped chewing his cuticles constantly.

·· • ● • ··

Paul and Mandy reconnected and resumed living as man and wife. Their extended family was happy about this except for their niece Molly who made a point of telling her uncle that he would regret his decision. Molly had recently been asked not to return to work at Hungry Jack's due to playing a practical joke on the manager, so she eventually came crawling back to Mandy because the agency her aunt worked for was advertising for temporary administration staff. It was the only agency left in Adelaide that Molly didn't have a bad reputation with *yet*. Certain people never grew up or took responsibility. Molly was one of them. Mandy bumped into Janet at the local shops a few weeks later. Janet gave a fake smile and feigned happiness about Mandy being reconciled with Paul. Stoney faced, Mandy retorted 'Cut the bullshit Janet, I'm on to you. Paul was not territory you should have been near and you know it.' Janet did not see the point in protesting her innocence, she knew she was busted. 'Yeah so what? He was a free agent so you can't say shit about it. I turned him down in the end anyway.' Janet sneered bitchily as she waited on Mandy's response.

Mandy knew instinctively that Janet was lying to be vindictive so she shook her head and turned on her heel to walk away from her friendship of ten years. It felt great. Until this happened she had not realised she had outgrown this woman and did not cherish her company any more. Janet gaped at Mandy's retreating back. *The cheek of the woman!* She did feel a prickle of guilt as it occurred to her that the story might get back to her husband but then she realised she probably couldn't get rid of the fat oaf if she tried. *Meh! What will be will be!* Not being one to suffer from a guilty conscience very often, Janet carried on browsing the shelves of her local Foodland as though nothing out of the ordinary had just happened.

CHAPTER 43

Alessandro's Cucina was declared a crime scene and was cordoned off while forensics swept through the restaurant for evidence. Alan was distraught. He assumed that his business would go down the drain as a result of the horrors that had occurred there. The insurance would cover certain costs, but loss of revenue was the wider issue. Although the investigations had pretty much concluded and it was clear-cut whom the perpetrator and the victims were, he couldn't help but feel an impending sense of doom about opening the restaurant doors to the public again. Surely the regular patrons would be too spooked to return?

News coverage about the couple who'd been shot dead in the restaurant was still all over every TV channel and their distraught family members had recently told their tragic story on *60 Minutes.* Alan watched nervously whilst peering anxiously through his hands. *Who in God's name will want to eat at the restaurant now? My business is screwed!*

The following day, Alan was incredulous to find out online that not only was there a GoFundMe page to raise money for loss of staff income and damages, but there were also several polls indicating that people couldn't *wait* to eat at Alessandro's Cucina!

Alan could not believe what he was reading. Instead of shunning the restaurant where the horrors had taken place, people wanted to come and have their photos taken there! Alan surmised that the world was a pretty strange place these days. It looked like sensationalism had finally taken over the world. Next, people would be taking selfies next to the Snowtown murder barrels.

Alan decided the restaurant needed a new look and when he finally got the all-clear from police, he had the restaurant revamped. He also signed up for Uber Eats deliveries. It looked like he had to keep up with the times if he wanted to make the best of a bad situation. While making the most of his good fortune but feeling somewhat disturbed by it, Alan concluded that these days, weird was the new normal.

Alan was glad to have his head waiter back on deck as Jagriti began making plans to open her own Indian restaurant with the backing of her parents. He was sad to see his best worker leave but supported her in her quest to follow her dreams. Alan was grateful that Jagriti had offered her wise counsel in the weeks following the siege. She had assured Alan that he was not to blame for placing her on the roster to work that night, that she was an adult who made her own decisions so he needed to stop torturing himself as he was not to blame for her ordeal. Eventually Alan came around to her way of thinking and stopped with the incessant guilt trip. He fully intended to be a regular customer at Jagriti's restaurant when it opened. It was the least he could do. Besides, he had tasted Keerti's butter chicken and could not stop licking his lips whenever he thought about it. Apparently, Jagriti had her mother's recipes down pat so he truly believed she had an exciting future ahead of her.

Rahul was obsessed with security following the siege and given he had to be in control of *something*, Jagriti allowed him to be in charge of the health and safety aspects of running her new restaurant. This would allow Rahul to watch live footage of staff working in the restaurant via the camera on his laptop. It was extreme, but if it would give him the peace of mind he craved then Jagriti was on board with it. It was kind of cute that he still wanted to make sure she was safe, although, given he was a busy GP, she was not quite sure how he could constantly monitor this. Jagriti knew that based on the balance of probabilities, it was unlikely she would ever face a second siege situation but Rahul was not a logical thinker despite how academic he was. Keerti secretly wanted to join Jagriti and work in the restaurant but she feared Rahul would not approve. One step at a time she surmised. First they would set their daughter up and then when she was a roaring success, they would tackle the next hurdle with Rahul. Sometimes the secret was to use reverse psychology and make him think it was his idea all along. His gripe would likely be that if Keerti was at work then she was not home to cook for him but when she told him that cooking at work meant she could bring all the left overs home, he would soon change his mind. Keerti smiled as she anticipated the bright future ahead of them all.

EPILOGUE

Once the hype had died down and the siege became yesterday's news, Marshall requested a private therapy session with Briony. When she consulted her electronic diary at 8.30am on a sunny Monday morning to ascertain the names of the officers she would be seeing that day, she was somewhat surprised to see that Marshall had booked in for the first appointment of the day.

Caught off guard, Briony quickly ran to the ladies' to make sure she was looking her best. After reapplying her red lipstick, she undid the messy bun piled on top of her head and shook her long blonde hair free so that it fell loosely on her shoulders. Then she undid the first two buttons on her blouse, quickly felt guilty for being deliberately seductive, and finally found a compromise by only leaving the top one open instead.

Normally she read up on the police officers she would be seeing to get a feel for their background and the areas they worked in. However, this was an unusual scenario where she'd had to rely on her assistant to book this week's appointments blindly for her. Briony had spread herself thin by attending an important conference interstate with the police psychologists from the other jurisdictions in Australia over the weekend. She was kicking herself for not knowing about Marshall booking in. She usually needed to prepare herself before meeting with him. No one ever suspected how she truly felt about him due to her ability to compose herself using psychobabble, which allowed her to slow her breathing around him.

Once back in her office, she tapped her pen impatiently on her desk. Marshall wasn't due for another ten minutes. She decided to use the time to check out the other names on her list. She noted with interest that the sniper who had taken the fatal shot to snuff out Farzad was also due to see her later that morning. She wasn't overly surprised. He had probably finally succumbed to the realisation that he had severe Post Traumatic Stress Disorder. Briony would put money on the fact that he was having nightmares and struggling to function at his job post-siege. Just as she was considering the best psychology methodologies for this situation, there was a sharp rap on her office door. She smiled. It was a familiar knock, and she knew straight away that it was Marshall. Briony took a deep breath and tried to ignore the fact that she felt more than a little horny.

Marshall gave himself a pep talk on the way to Briony's office. *Keep it professional, don't just blurt it all out.*

The minute that Marshall sat in the plush leather chair, he felt silly and questioned if he'd done the right thing by coming to see her. *She is professional, genuinely cares and is the only one I can trust to maintain confidentiality – that's why I'm here.*

Briony tried to remain impassive. She had no clue why he'd come. After a few false starts where he'd tried to stick to small talk, Briony pointed at her watch and said, 'You have forty minutes left to get to the point. I suggest you use them wisely.'

Marshall cleared his throat. 'I caught my wife in bed with a female officer,' he mumbled, his eyes downcast. Briony nodded for him to continue, her face giving nothing away. *Oh God, he finally found out! His ego is clearly hurt but I'm glad it's out in the open and I'm not burdened with knowing about it any longer.*

Briony paused, waiting for him to ask her how to take the pain away. Marshall stood up and looked out of the window. Men often did this to avoid eye contact with her when uncomfortable during therapy sessions.

'Take your time,' she said evenly. Briony was quickly processing what this must mean for him and wondered if he was delusional enough to think that he could win his wife back. She was fully aware of how long the affair had been going on. It certainly wasn't just an experiment with the same sex for the hell of it.

'She's gone, and I'm glad,' Marshall said quietly. He sat back in the chair and took a deep breath. 'Okay, I will come out with it. I was initially upset but then realised we were never genuinely happy in our marriage. We had a frank discussion about it, and we are parting on good terms. There's a sense of relief for us both.'

Briony frowned, confusion etched on her face. She had not expected him to be so cool about it. *Why is he here for therapy if he is fine with it?* she pondered.

Marshall finally looked her straight in the eye. 'I realised that it was you I wanted for all these years. We were both so proud and neither of us admitted it … tell me I'm right?' *Shit, I can't believe I just said that. It wasn't part of the plan.* A bead of sweat formed on his upper lip, a sure giveaway that he was nervous.

Briony gaped at him, speechless for once in her life. Her head was saying, *this is not appropriate or professional and no matter how I feel, I can't lose all credibility as a psychologist by going along with this.* On the other hand, her heart was saying, *I never realised how much I wanted to hear those words until he finally said them.*

To her horror, she realised her body was responding to his words, her stiff nipples evident through her flimsy blouse. Marshall stood up and to her relief, he walked towards the door. *He is going to do the right thing and leave before we embarrass each other further.*

Briony's head snapped up as she heard Marshall turn the key in the lock of her office door. He walked slowly back towards her. She felt powerless to stop him. He stood in front of her, unbuttoning her blouse whilst nibbling her neck and she quickly found his zipper to free his bulging erection. They frantically stripped each other and had urgent, rough sex on her desk. They lost track of time until Briony's desk phone buzzed to let her know her next client was there.

In a panic, Marshall and Briony threw their clothes back on, both cursing that they had been so careless and perilously close to being caught out.

When a dishevelled looking Marshall left Briony's office and a flushed, tousled-haired Briony greeted the sniper who'd arrived for his session, he was quick to put two and two together. When, for the first time in her career, Briony vagued out with a dreamy look on her face during a client session, the sniper became mighty pissed off and quickly spread a rumour around the police force exaggerating what he had seen.

When Marshall and Briony were hauled across the coals and questioned by their superiors, they both came clean and admitted they were in love.

They were both brilliant at their jobs and would be too much of a loss if they made an example of them by moving them to other units; however, their relationship was a clear code of conduct issue. Finally, Marshall took a position in the country to appease his boss and commenced divorce proceedings. Two years later, he and Briony were married in the Maldives and only then did they both finally stop thinking about the siege.

ACKNOWLEDGMENTS

Thank you to everyone who bought my first novel *Hidden From View*. I am incredibly grateful and humbled by the sales and reviews, given that I was a first-time author. I am constantly learning and growing as a writer and love hearing readers' thoughts on my work so please keep up the reviews and contact via my social media platforms: Facebook (Gill D Anderson author), Instagram (gillyanderson71) and more recently Twitter (@GillianAnders16). Once again, I would like to thank the fabulous team at InHouse Publishing for their wonderful service, professional advice and their collective wisdom.